Happy Christmas Emma.
1989

True Confessions
of Adrian Albert Mole
Margaret Hilda Roberts
and Susan Lilian Townsend

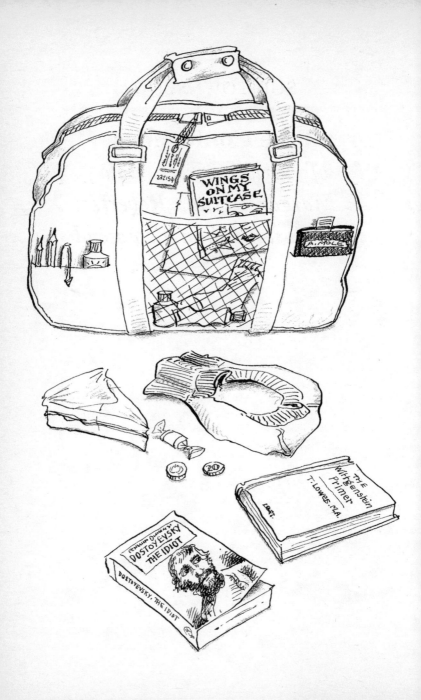

SUE TOWNSEND

True Confessions
of *Adrian Albert Mole*
Margaret Hilda Roberts
and Susan Lilian Townsend

METHUEN

by the same author

FICTION
The Secret Diary of Adrian Mole
The Growing Pains of Adrian Mole
Rebuilding Coventry
The Secret Diary of Adrian Mole Song Book
(in collaboration with Ken Howard and Alan Blaikley)

PLAYS
Bazaar and Rummage, Groping for Words, Womberang
The Great Celestial Cow
The Secret Diary of Adrian Mole (the play)

*The line drawings in this book
are by Caroline Holden*

First published in 1989
by Methuen London
Michelin House, 81 Fulham Road, London SW3 6RB
Copyright © 1984, 1985, 1986, 1987,
1988, 1989 by Sue Townsend

A CIP catalogue record for this book
is available from the British Library
ISBN 0 413 62450 1

Acknowledgements
Some of the pieces in this book
have previously appeared in the following
publications: *Airport*; *Arts of the Earth*;
The Guardian; *Punch*; *New Statesman*; *News on Sunday*;
Spitting Image Christmas Book; *Sunday Telegraph*;
The Times; *Woman*; *Woman's Realm*.
Mole on Pirate Radio 4 was broadcast BBC Radio 4.

Printed in Great Britain
by Richard Clay Ltd, Bungay, Suffolk

To Lin Hardcastle
childhood friend

Contents

Author's Preface

Dearest reader,

Since the scandal broke about the so called 'five dwarves in a bed' affair (though I still maintain there were only four) I have seldom visited civilisation; my meagre supplies are delivered to me by donkey carrier every second Tuesday. I collect peat from the moors for my fire and I draw water from a well conveniently situated only three miles from my cottage. Thus my needs are satisfied.

What care I for the trappings of success? What joy did I ever get from wearing *Joy* perfume? None – only more mosquito bites when I went abroad.

The occasional visitor brings me news of London's vibrant literary scene. Sometimes they bring commissions; it is by this method that I finance my chosen frugal life style. This book is a collection of some of the articles and essays I have written over the past few years.

There is also some previously unpublished material, *The Prison Letters* between A. Mole and Barry Kent, for example. And some poetry written by A. Mole (included here only because he threatened to starve himself to death unless I agreed).

Mole's blackmailing tactics have succeeded to the extent that he has the lion's share of this book, though I must stress that this is not a 'Mole book'; Margaret Hilda Roberts and I also contribute.

Old Hag Cottage
Top-O-Hill
Black Moor
Nr Buxton
April 1989

Notes on The Contributors

Adrian Albert Mole. Adrian Albert Mole was the editor and main contributor to the Neil Armstrong Comprehensive School magazine, *The Voice of Youth*.

Since then his poems have appeared in the *Leicester Mercury* and the *Skegness Herald*. A volume of his poems entitled *The Restless Tadpole* was printed by Vanity Publishers Ltd, in 1987.

He is currently writing a novel about the East Midlands called *Lo! the Flat Hills of My Homeland*.

Adrian Mole lives in Leicester with his dog. In 1986 he won record damages against the failed novelist Sue Townsend after she published his diaries claiming that they were her own works of fiction.

Margaret Hilda Roberts. These diary entries were found between the pages of *The Be-Ro Cook Book for Girls* at a car boot sale in Grantham on a Bank Holiday Monday in 1988.

Nothing (unfortunately) is known about Margaret Hilda Roberts or what became of her. The diary is believed to have been written in the nineteen thirties.

Susan Lilian Townsend. Enjoyed notoriety at one time but has sunk into obscurity since her involvement in the 'five dwarves in a bed' scandal in 1989 for which she received a suspended prison sentence of two years. The judge's remarks were widely reported in the popular press: 'To think that a woman of your age could stoop so low.'

Since the scandal she has lived in isolation in a bleak moorland cottage near to Buxton. She alleges that her only companions are a family of curlews and a large fungus growing in the corner of her living room. She is forty-three.

Adrian Albert Mole

Adrian Mole's Christmas

Monday   December 24th
CHRISTMAS EVE

Something dead strange has happened to Christmas. It's just not the same as it used to be when I was a kid. In fact I've never really got over the trauma of finding out that my parents had been lying to me annually about the existence of Santa Claus.

To me then, at the age of eleven, Santa Claus was a bit like God, all-seeing, all-knowing, but without the lousy things that God allows to happen: earthquakes, famines, motorway crashes. I would lie in bed under the blankets (how crude the word blankets sounds today when we are all conversant with the Tog rating of continental quilts), my heart pounding and palms sweaty in anticipation of the virgin *Beano* album. I would imagine big jolly Santa looking from his celestial sledge over our cul-de-sac and saying to his elves: 'Give Adrian Mole something decent this year. He is a good lad. He never forgets to put the lavatory seat down.' Ah . . . the folly of the child!

Alas, now at the age of maturity, (sixteen years, eight months and twenty-two days, five hours and six minutes) . . . I know that my parents walk around the town centre wild-eyed with consumer panic chanting desperately, 'What shall we get for Adrian?' Is it any wonder that Christmas Eve has lost its awe?

2.15am   Just got back from the Midnight Service. As usual it dragged on far too long. My mother started getting fidgety after the first hour of the co-op young wives' carols. She kept whispering, 'I shall have to go home soon or that bloody turkey will never be thawed out for the morning.'

Once again the Nativity Playlet was ruined by having a live donkey in the church. It never behaves itself, and always causes a major disturbance, so why does the vicar inflict it on us? O K so his brother-in-law runs a donkey sanctuary, but so what?

To be fair, the effect of the Midnight Service was dead moving. Even to me who is a committed nihilistic existentialist.

Tuesday   December 25th
CHRISTMAS DAY

Not a bad collection of presents considering my Dad's redundant. I got the grey zip-up cardigan I asked for. My mother said, 'If you want to look like a sixteen-year old Frank Bough then go ahead and wear the thing!'

The Oxford Dictionary will come in useful for increasing my word power. But the best present of all was the electric shaver. I have already had three shaves. My shin is as smooth as a billiard ball. Somebody should get one for Leon Brittain. It is not good for Britain's image for a cabinet minister to go around looking like a gangster who has been in the cells of a New York Police Station all night.

The lousy Sugdens, my mother's inbred Norfolk relations, turned up at 11.30am. So I got my parents out of bed and then retired to my room to read my *Beano* annual. Perhaps I am too worldly and literate nowadays, but I was quite disappointed at its childish level of humour.

I emerged from my room in time for Christmas dinner and was forced to engage the Sugdens in conversation. They told me in minute, mind-boggling detail, about the life-cycle of King Edward potatoes, from tuber to chip pan. They were not a bit interested in my conversation about the Norwegian Leather Industry. In fact they looked bored. Just my luck to have philistines for relations. Dinner was late as usual. My mother has never learnt the secret of co-ordinating the ingredients of a meal. Her gravy is always made before the roast potatoes have turned brown. I went into the kitchen to give her some advice, but she shouted, 'Bugger off out' through the steam. When it came the meal was quite nice but there was no witty repartee over the table; not a single hilarious anecdote was told. In fact I wish I'd had my Xmas dinner with Ned Sherrin. His relations are dead lucky to have him. I bet their sides ache from laughing.

The Sugdens don't approve of drink, so every time my parents even *looked* at a bottle of spirits they tightened their lips and sipped their tea. (And yes it *is* possible to do both, I've seen it with my own eyes.) In the evening we all had a desultory game of cards. Grandad Sugden won four thousand pounds off my father. There was a lot of joking about my father giving Grandad Sugden an IOU but father said to me in the kitchen, 'No way am I putting my name to paper, that mean old git would have me in court as fast as you could say King Edward!'

The Sugdens went to bed early on our rusty camp beds. They are leaving for Norfolk at dawn because they are worried about potato poachers. I now know why my mother turned out to be wilful and prone to alcohol abuse. It is a reaction against her lousy moronic upbringing in the middle of the potato fields of Norfolk.

Wednesday   December 26th
BOXING DAY

I was woken at dawn by the sound of Grandad Sugden's rusty Ford Escort refusing to start. I know I should have gone down into the street and helped to push it but Grandma Sugden seemed to be doing all right on her own. It must be all those years of flinging sacks of potatoes about. My parents were wisely pretending to be asleep, but I know they were awake because I could hear coarse laughter coming from their bedroom, and when the Sugdens' engine came alive and the Escort finally turned the corner of our cul-de-sac I distinctly heard the sound of a champagne cork popping and the chink of glasses. Not to mention the loud 'Cheers'.

Went back to sleep but the dog licked me awake at 9.30, so I took it for a walk past Pandora's house. Her dad's Volvo wasn't in the drive so they must still be staying with their rich relations. On the way I passed Barry Kent, who was kicking a football up against the wall of the old people's home. He seemed full of seasonal good will for once and I stopped to talk with him. He asked what I'd had for Christmas; I told him and I asked him what he'd had. He looked embarrassed and said, 'I ain't 'ad much this year 'cos our dad's lost his job'. I asked him what happened, he said, 'I dunno. Our dad says Mrs Thatcher took it off him.' I said 'What, personally?' Barry shrugged and said, 'Well that's what our dad reckons.'

Barry asked me back to his house for a cup of tea so I went to show that I bore him no grudge from the days when he used to demand money with menaces from me. The outside of the Kents' council house looked very grim. (Barry told me that the council have been promising to mend the fences, doors and windows for years) but the inside looked magical. Paper chains were hung everywhere, almost completely hiding the cracks in the walls and ceilings. Mr Kent had been out into the community and found a large branch, painted it with white gloss paint and stuck it into the empty paint tin. This branch effectively took the place of a Christmas tree in my opinion, but Mrs Kent said, sadly, 'But it's not the same really, not if the only reason you've got it is because you can't afford to have a real, plastic one.' I was going to say that their improvised tree was modernistic and Hi Tech but I kept my mouth shut.

I asked the Kent children what they'd had for Christmas and they said, 'Shoes.' So I had to pretend to admire them. I had no choice because they kept sticking them under my nose. Mrs Kent laughed and said, 'And Mr Kent and me gave each other a packet of fags!' As you know, dear diary, I disapprove of smoking but I could understand their need to have a bit of pleasure at Christmas so I didn't give them my anti-smoking lecture.

I didn't like to ask any more questions and politely declined the mince pies they offered . . . from where I was sitting I could see into their empty pantry.

Walking back home I wondered how my parents were able to buy decent Christmas presents for me. After all my father and

Mr Kent were both innocent victims of the robot culture where machines are preferred to people.

As I came through our back door I found out. My father was saying, 'But how the hell am I going to pay the next Access bill, Pauline?' My mother said, 'We'll have to sell something George, whatever happens we've got to hang on to at least one credit card because it's impossible to live on the dole and social security!'

So my family's Christmas prosperity is a thin veneer. We've had it on credit.

In the afternoon we went round to Grandma's for Boxing Day tea. As she slurped out the trifle she complained bitterly about her Christmas Day spent at the Evergreen Club. She said, 'I knew I shouldn't have gone; that filthy communist Bert Baxter got disgustingly drunk on a box of liqueur chocolates and sang crude words at the Carol Service!'

My father said, 'You should have come to us, mum, I did ask you!'

Grandma said, 'You only asked me *once* and anyway the Sugdens were there.' This last remark offended my mother; she is always criticising her family but she hates anybody else to do the same. The tea ended in disaster when I broke a willow pattern plate that Grandma has had for years. I know Grandma loves me but I have to record that on this occasion she looked at me with murder in her eyes. She said, 'Nobody will ever know what that plate meant to me!' I offered to pick the pieces up but she pushed me away with the end of the hand brush. I went into the bathroom to cool down. After twenty minutes my mother banged on the door and said, 'C'mon, Adrian, we're going home. Grandma's just told your dad that it's his own fault he's been made redundant.' As I passed through the living room the silence between my father and my Grandma was as solid as a double-glazed window.

As we passed Pandora's house in the car, I saw that the fairy lights on the fir tree in her garden were switched on, so I asked my parents to drop me off. Pandora was ecstatic to see me at first. She raved about the present I bought her (a solid gold bracelet from Tesco's, £2.49) but after a while she cooled a bit and started going on about the Christmas house-party she'd been to. She made a lot of references to a boy called Crispin Wartog-Lowndes. Apparently he is an expert rower and he rowed Pandora across a lake on Christmas day. Whilst doing so he quoted from the works of Percy Bysshe Shelley. According to Pandora there was a mist on the lake. I got into a silent jealous rage and imagined pushing Crispin Wartog-Lowndes's aristocratic face under the lake until he'd forgotten about Pandora, Christmas and Shelley. I got into bed at 1am, worn out with all the emotion. In fact, as I lay in the dark, tears came to my eyes; especially when I remembered the Kents' empty pantry.

The Mole/Mancini Letters

From
Hamish Mancini
196 West Houston Street
New York, N.Y.

Hi there Aidy!
How are you kid? . . . How's the zits . . . your face still
look like the surface of the moon? Hey don't worry, I
gotta cure. You rub the corpse of a dead frog into your
face at night. Do you have frogs in England? . . . Your
mum gotta blender? . . . OK, here's what you do:

1. You find a dead frog.
2. You put it in the blender. (Gory, but you don't have to
   look.)
3. You depress the button for 30 seconds. (Neither do you
   have to listen.)
4. You pour the resulting gunk into a jar.
5. You wash the blender, huh?
6. Last thing at night (clean your teeth *first*) you apply the
   gunk to your face. It works! I now gotta complexion like

a baby's ass. Hey! It was great reading your diary, even
the odd unflattering remark about me. Still, old buddy,
I forgive you on account of how you were of unsound
mind at the time you wrote the stuff. An' I got
questions . . .

1. What does RSPCA stand for?
2. Who's Malcolm Muggeridge?
3. For chrissake, what are PE shorts?
4. Is the *Morning Star* a commie newspaper?
5. Where's Skegness? . . . What's Skegness rock?
6. 'V' sign? . . . Like Churchill the war leader?
7. Toad in the Hole, is it food or what?
8. Woodbines? . . . Bert Baxter smokes flowers?
9. Family Allowance . . . is this a charity handout?
10. Kevin Keegan . . . who is he?
11. Barclaycard . . . what is it?
12. Yorkshire Puddings . . . what are they?
13. Broadcasting House?
14. How much in dollars is 25 pence?
15. Is a Mars Bar candy?
16. Is Sainsbury's a hypermarket?
17. What's the PDSA, some kinda animal hospital?
18. GCEs, what *are* they?
19. Think I can guess what *Big and Bouncy* magazine is
    like . . . but gimme some *details*, kid?
20. Bovril – sounds disgusting! . . . Is it?
21. Evergreens? . . . Explain please.
22. Social Services?
23. Spotted Dick . . . jeezus! . . . This some sexual disease?
24. Is a 'detention centre' jail?
25. You bought your mother 'Black Magic' – what is she,
    a witch or something?
26. Where's Sheffield?
27. What's Habitat?
28. Radio Four, is it some local station?
29. O' level what?
30. What is a copper's nark?
31. Noddy? That the goon in the little car?
32. Dole . . . 'Social Security' . . . is this like our Welfare?

33. Sir Edmund Hilary . . . he a relation of yours?
34. Alma Cogan . . . she a singer?
35. Lucozade . . . did you get drunk?
36. What's a conker?
37. The dog is AWOL . . . what is or was AWOL?
38. Who is or was Noel Coward?
39. What is BUPA?
40. What are 'wellingtons'?
41. Who is Tony Benn?
42. Petrol . . . you mean gas?
43. Is *The Archers* a radio serial about Robin Hood?
44. Is the Co-op a commie-run store?
45. Is VAT a kinda tax?
46. *Eating* a chapati? . . . Isn't chapati French for hat?
47. Rouge? . . . Don't you mean blusher?
48. Is an Alsatian a German Shepherd?
49. What's a Rasta?

Send info back soonest,
Yours eagerly, your old buddy
    Hamish

PS. Mum's in the Betty Ford Clinic.
She's doin' OK, they've cured everything but the
kleptomania.

Leicester
February 1st 1985

Dear Hamish,
Thanks for your long letter but please try to put postage
stamps on the envelope next time you write. You are rich
and I am poor, I cannot afford to subsidise your
scribblings. You owe me twenty-six pence. Please send it
immediately.

I am no *so* desperate about my complexion that I have
to resort to covering my face with purée of frog. In fact,
Hamish, I was repelled and disgusted by your advice, and
anyway my mother *hasn't* got a blender. She has stopped

cooking entirely. My father and I forage for ourselves as best we can. I'm pleased that you enjoyed reading my diary even though many of the references were unfamiliar to you. I am enclosing a glossary for your edification.

1. RSPCA stands for: the Royal Society for the Prevention of Cruelty to Animals.
2. Malcolm Muggeridge: is an old intellectual who is always on TV. A bit like Gore Vidal, only more wrinkles.
3. PE shorts: running shorts as worn in Physical Education.
4. Yes, the *Morning Star* is a communist newspaper.
5. Skegness is a proletarian sea-side resort. Skegness rock is tubular candy.
6. 'V' sign: it means . . . get stuffed!
7. Toad in the hole: a batter pudding containing sausages.
8. Woodbines: small, lethally strong cigarettes.
9. Family Allowance: a small government payment made to parents of all children.
10. Kevin Keegan: a genius footballer now retired.
11. Barclaycard: plastic credit card.
12. Yorkshire Puddings: batter puddings minus sausages.
13. Broadcasting House: headquarters of the BBC.
14. Work it out for yourself.
15. Mars Bars: yes, it's candy, and very satisfying it is too.
16. Sainsbury's: is where teachers, vicars and suchlike do their food shopping.
17. PDSA: People's Dispensary for Sick Animals. A place where poor people take their ill animals.
18. GCEs are exams.
19. *Big and Bouncy:* a copy is on its way to you. Hide it from your mum.
20. Bovril: is a nourishing meat extract drink.
21. Evergreens: a club for wrinklies over 65 years.
22. Social Services: government agency to help the unfortunate, the unlucky, and the poor.
23. Spotted Dick: is a suet pudding containing sultanas. I find your sexual innuendos about my favourite pudding offensive in the extreme.

24. Detention Centre: jail for teenagers.
25. Black Magic: dark chocolates.
26. Sheffield: refer to map.
27. Habitat: store selling cheap, fashionable furniture.
28. Radio Four: BBC-run channel, bringing culture, news and art to Britain's listening masses.
29. O' level: see GCE's.
30. Copper's nark: rat fink who gives the police information about criminal activity.
31. Noddy: fictional figure from childhood. I hate his guts.
32. Dole: Social Security: yes, it's Welfare.
33. Sir Edmund Hilary: first bloke to climb Everest.
34. Alma Cogan: singer, now alas dead.
35. Lucozade: non-alcoholic drink. Invalids guzzle it.
36. Conker: round shiny brown nut. The fruit of the horse chestnut. British children thread string through them, and then engage in combat by smashing one conker against another. The kid whose conker gets smashed loses.
37. AWOL: British Army expression. It means absent without leave.
38. Noel Coward: wit, singer, playwright, actor, songwriter. Ask your mother, she probably *knew* him.
39. BUPA: private medicine, a bit like the Blue Cross.
40. Wellingtons: rubber boots. The queen wears them.
41. Tony Benn: an ex-aristocrat, now a fervent Socialist politician.
42. Petrol: OK . . . OK . . . gas.
43. The Archers: a radio serial about English countryfolk.
44. The Co-op: a grocery chain run on Socialist principles.
45. VAT: a tax. The scourge of small businesses.
46. Chapati: *not* a French hat. It's a flat Indian bread!
47. Rouge: *you* can call it blusher if you like. *I* call it *rouge*.
48. Alsatian: yes, also called German Shepherd, terrifying whatever they're called.
49. Rasta: a member of the Rastafarian religion. Members are usually black. Wear their hair in dreadlocks (plaits) and smoke illegal substances. They have complicated handshakes.

Look Hamish, I'm at the end of my patience now. If there is anything else you cannot understand please refer to the reference books. Ask your mother or any passing Anglophile. And please! . . . please! . . . send my diaries back. I would hate them to fall into unfriendly, possible commercial hands. I am afraid of blackmail; as you know my diaries are full of sex and scandal. Please for the sake of our continuing friendship . . . send my diaries back!

I remain, Hamish,

Your trusting, humble and obedient servant and friend.

A. Mole

A Letter to the BBC

Leicester
February 14th

Dear Mr Tydeman,
I am sending you, as requested, my latest poem. Please
write back by return of post if you wish to broadcast the
said poem. Our telephone has been disconnected (again).
  I remain, Sir, your most humble and obedient servant,
    A. Mole

Throbbing

Pandora,
I am but young
I am but small
(with cratered skin)
Yet! Hear my call.

Oh, rapturous girl
With skin sublime
Whose favourite programme's 'Question Time'
Look over here
To where I stand
A throbbing
Like a swollen gland.

A Mole

Adrian Mole on 'Pirate Radio Four'

Art Culture and Politcs

August 1985

I would like to thank the BBC for inviting me to talk to you on Radio 4. It's about time they had a bit of culture on in the morning. Before I begin properly I'd just like to take this opportunity to reassure my parents that I got here safely.

Hello, Mum. Hello, Dad. The train was OK. Second Class was full so I went into First Class and sat down and pretended to be a lunatic. Fortunately the ticket inpsector has got a lunatic in his family so he was quite sympathetic and took me to sit on a stool in the guard's van. As you know I am normally an introvert, so pretending to be a lunatic extrovert for an hour and twenty minutes wore me out, and I was glad when the train steamed into the cavernous monolith that is St Pancras station. Well to be quite honest the train didn't steam in because as you, Dad, will know, steam has been phased out and is now but an erotic memory in a train spotter's head.

Anyway I got a taxi like you told me, a black one with a high roof. I got in and said, 'Take me to the BBC'. The driver said, 'Which BBC?' in a surly sort of tone. I *nearly* said, 'I don't like your tone my man', but I bit my tongue back and explained: 'I'm speaking on Radio Four this morning'. He said, 'Good job you ain't goin' on the telly wiv your face.' He must have been referring to the bits of green toilet paper sticking to my shaving cuts. I didn't know what to say to his cruel remark, so I kept quiet and watched the money clock like you told me to do. You won't believe it, Mum, but it cost me two pounds forty-five pence! ... I know ... incredible isn't it? Two pounds forty-five pence! I gave him two pound notes and a fifty pence piece and told him to keep the change. I can't repeat what *he* said because this is Radio Four and not Radio Three but he flung his five pence tip into the gutter and drove off shouting horrible things. I grovelled in the gutter for ages, but you'll be pleased to hear that I found the five pence.

A bloke in a general's uniform barred my way to the hallowed portals of Broadcasting House. He said, 'And whom might you be sunshine?' I said quite coldly (because once again I didn't care for his tone), 'I am Adrian Mole, the Diarist and Juvenile Philosopher'. He turned to another general ... in fact, thinking about it, it could have been the *Director* General because this second general looked sort of noble yet careworn. Anyway, the first general shouted, 'Look on the list under Mole will you ...?' The second general replied (in cultivated tones, so it must have been the Director General) 'Yes I've got a Mole on the list ... Studio B 198'. Before I knew it, a wizened-up old guide appeared at my elbow and showed me into a palatial lift. Then, once out of the lift – which was twice as big as my bedroom by the way – he took me down tortured, turning corridors. It was like George Orwell's Ministry of Truth in that book called *1984*. No wonder DJs are always late turning up for work.

Eventually, exhausted and panting, we arrived outside the door of studio B 198. I was a bit worried about the old guide. To tell you the truth I thought he'd force me to give him mouth to mouth, such was his feeble condition. I really think that the BBC ought to provide oxygen on each floor for their older employees; and a trained nurse wouldn't be a bad idea either. It would save them money in the long run; they wouldn't have to keep replacing staff all the time and collecting for wreaths and things. Anyway, just thought I'd tell you that I got here all right. Oh, you know the BBC bloke I've been writing to, that producer John Tydeman.

Well he's dead scruffy. He looks like he *writes*. You know, with a beard and heavy horn-rimmed glasses. Need I say more? I'd better stop talking to you now Mum and Dad, because he's making crude signs at me through the glass – so much for the standard of education at the BBC!

Oh, before I forget, did you send that excuse to Pop-Eye Scruton telling him that I've gone down with an 'as yet unnamed' virus? If not, can you take one to school immediately after my broadcast? . . . Thanks, only, as you know, he refused me permission to come here today. How mean can you get? Fancy denying one of the foremost intellectuals in school the opportunity to talk about art and culture on the BBC. You'll be sure to mark the envelope 'for the attention of the Headmaster' won't you Dad? Don't forget and put 'Pop-Eye Scruton' on, like you did last time.

Well I'd better start properly now . . . I've got my notes somewhere . . . (*pause . . . rustling . . .*) Oh dear . . . I've left them in the taxi. Oh well, it's quite lucky that I'm good at doing 'ad hoc' spontaneous talking isn't it? . . . So, Art and Culture. Are they important?

Well, I think Art and Culture *are* important. *Dead* important. Without Art and Culture we would descend to the level of animals who aimlessly fill their time by hanging around dustbins and getting into fights. The people who don't allow Art and Culture into their lives can always be spotted. They are pale from watching too much television, and also their conversation lacks a certain *je ne sais quoi*; unless they are French of course. Cultureless people talk about the price of turnips and why bread always falls on the buttered side, and other such inane things. You never hear them mention Van Gogh or Rembrandt or Bacon (by Bacon, I'm talking about Francis Bacon the infamous artist, I don't mean streaky bacon or Danish bacon . . . the sort you eat). No, such names mean nothing to cultureless people, they will never pilgrimage to the Louvre Museum to see Michaelangelo's Mona Lisa. Nor will they thrill to a Brahms Opera. They will fill their empty days with frivolous frivolity, and eventually die never having tasted the sweet ambrosia of culture.

I therefore feel it incumbent upon me to promote artisticness wherever I tread. If I meet a low-browed person I force them into a philosophical conversation. I ask them, 'Why are we here?' Often their answers are facetious. For instance last week I asked a humble market trader that very question. He answered, 'I dunno why you're 'ere mate but I'm 'ere to flog carrots'.

Such people are to be pitied. We of superior intellect must not judge them too harshly, but gently nudge them into the direction of the theatre rather than the betting shop. The art gallery instead of the bingo hall. The local madrigal society as opposed to the discotheque. I know that there are cynics who say 'England is governed by philistines, so what do you expect?' but to those cynics I say yes, we may be governed by philistines at the moment but I'd like to take this opportunity to talk about a political party that I've started up. It is called the Mole Move-ment. As yet we are small, but one day our influence will be felt throughout our land. Who knows, one day our party could be the party of government. I could end up as Prime Minister. Is it so inconceivable? Not in my opinion. Mrs Thatcher was once a humble housewife and mother. So, if she can do it, why can't I?

The 'Mole Movement' was formed on Boxing Day 1985. You know what it's like on Boxing Day. You've opened the presents, you've eaten all the white meat on the turkey, your half-witted relations are bickering about Aunt Ethel's will, and why Norman didn't deserve to get the scabby old clock: a general feeling of *ennui* (*ennui* is French for bored out of your skull by the way). Yes, *ennui* hangs around the house like stale fag smoke. Anyway it was Boxing Day and my girlfriend, Pandora Braithwaite, had come round so that we could exchange belated Christmas greet-ings. Her family took her to stay in a hotel for Christmas because Mrs Braithwaite said that if she had to stare up the rear of another turkey she would go berserk.

Anyway, we exchanged presents; I gave her a fish ash tray I made in pottery at school, and she gave me a Marks and Spencers voucher so that I could replace my old underpants. The elastic's gone . . . yes . . . so we thanked each other and kissed for about five minutes. I didn't want us to get carried away and end up as single parents . . . not in our A' level year. It wouldn't be fair to the kid with us both studying . . . er . . . what did I start to . . .? Yes. Well, after the kissing stopped I started to talk about my aspirations, and Pandora smoked one of her stinking French fags and listened to me with grave attention. I spoke passionately about beauty and elegance, and bringing back the old branch lines on the railways. I thundered against tower blocks and leisure centres, and ended by saying 'Pandora, my love, will you join me in my Life's Work?' Pandora moved languidly on my bed and said, 'You haven't said what your life's work is yet, *chéri*'.

I stood over her and said, 'Pandora, my life's work is the pursuit of beauty over ugliness, of truth over deceit, and of justice over rich people hogging all the money'. Pandora ran to the bathroom and was violently sick, such was the dramatic effect my speech had on her. To tell the truth I was a bit misty-eyed myself, and while she was throwing up I studied my face in the wardrobe mirror and definitely saw a change for the better. For where once was adolescent uncertainty was now mature complacency.

Pandora emerged from the bathroom and said 'My God, darling, I don't know what's going to happen to you'. I pulled her into my arms and reassured her about my future. I said, 'The way ahead may be stony but I will walk it barefoot if necessary'. Our oblique conversation was interrupted by my mother making mundane enquiries about how many spoons of sugar Pandora took in her cocoa. After my mother had stamped off down the stairs I turned in despair and cried, 'Oh save me from the *petit bourgeoisie* with their inane enquiries about beverages'. We tried to continue the conversation but it was again interrupted when my father went into the bathroom and started making disgusting grunting noises. He is so uncouth! . . . He can't wash his face without sounding like two warthogs mating in a watering hole. How I managed to spring from his loins I'll never know. In fact sometimes I think that it wasn't *his* loins I sprang from; my mother was once very friendly with a poet. Not a full time poet: he was a maggot farmer during the day, but at night, after the maggots had been shut up in their sheds, he would pull a pad of Basildon Bond towards him and write poems. Quite good poems as well; one of them got into the local paper. My mother cut it out and kept it . . . surely the action of a woman in love. When my mother came in with the cocoa I quizzed her about her relationship with the maggot poet. 'Oh Ernie Crabtree?' she said, pretending innocence. 'Yes', I said, then went on with heavy emphasis: 'I am like him in many ways aren't I . . .? The poetry for instance'. My mother said, 'You're nothing like him. He was witty and clever and unconventional and he made me laugh. Also he was six foot tall and devastatingly handsome'.

'So why didn't you marry him?' I asked. My mother sighed and sat down on my bed next to Pandora. 'Well, I couldn't stand the maggots. In the end I gave him an ultimatum. "Ernie", I said, "It's me or the maggots. You must choose between us." And he chose the maggots.' Her lips started to tremble and so I left the room and bumped into my father on the landing. By now I was determined to sort out my paternity so I quizzed him about Ernie Crabtree. 'Yeah, Ernie's done well for himself', he said. 'They call him the Maggot King in fishing circles. He's got a chain of maggot farms now and a mansion with a pack of Dobermans running in the grounds ... yeah, good old Ernie.' 'Does he still write poetry?' I enquired. 'Listen, son', said my father, and bent so close that I could see his thirty-year-old acne scars. 'Listen, Ernie's bank statements are pure poetry. He doesn't need to *write* the stuff.' My father got into bed, took his vest off and reached for the best-selling book he was reading. (Myself I never read best-sellers on principle. It's a good rule of thumb. If the masses like it then I'm sure that I won't.)

'Dad', I said, 'what did Ernie Crabtree look like?' My father cracked the spine of his book open, lit a disgusting fag and said 'Short fat bloke with a glass eye, wore a ginger wig ... now clear off, I'm reading'. I went back to my room to find Pandora and my mother having one of those sickening talks that women have nowadays. It was full of words like 'unfulfilled', 'potential', and 'identity'. Pandora kept chipping in with 'environment' and 'socio-economic' and 'chauvinistic attitude'. I got my pyjamas out of my drawer, signalling that I wished their conversation to desist, but neither of them took the hint so I was forced to change in the bathroom. When I came back the air was full of French cigarette smoke, and they were gassing about the Common Market and the relevance of something called 'milk quotas'.

I hung about tidying my desk and folding my clothes, but eventually I was forced to climb into bed while the conversation continued on either side of me. When they got on to cruise missiles I was forced to intercept and plead for a bit of multilateral peace.

Fortunately the dog got into a fight with a gang of dogs outside in the street so my mother was forced to run outside and separate it from the other canines with a mop handle. I took this opportunity to speak to Pandora. I said, 'While you may have been idly chatting with my mother I have been formulating important ideas. I have decided that I am going to have a party.' Pandora said, 'A fancy dress party?' 'No', I shouted, 'I'm forming a *political* party, well more of a Movement, really. It will be called the Mole Movement and membership will be £2 a year. Pandora asked what she would get for £2 a year. I replied, 'Arresting conversation and stimulation and stuff'. She opened her mouth to ask another question so I closed my eyes and feigned sleep. I heard the squelch of Pandora's moon boots as she tip-toed to the door, opened it and went off, squelching, down the stairs. Thus was the 'Mole Movement' born.

The next morning, I woke with an epic poem thundering inside my head. Even before I had cleaned my teeth I was at my desk scribbling feverishly. I was interrupted once when a visitor called from Matlock, but I declined the encyclopaedias he was selling, and returned to my desk. The poem was finished at 11.35am Greenwich Mean Time. And this is it.

THE HOI POLLOI RECEPTION
BY A. MOLE

The food stood on the table
The drink stood on the bar
The crisps lay in the glass dish
'Twixt the gherkins in the jar.
The poets were expected
The artists had sent word
The pianists and flautists
Were bringing lemon curd.

The novelists were travelling
From dim and distant lands
The journalists were trekking
O'er deep and shifting sands.
The *hoi polloi* stood standing
Outside the party room
Which glowed with invitation

Like a twenty-year-old womb.
Yet they dared not cross the portal
To taste the waiting feast
For fear of what would happen
If they dared to cross the beast.

The *hoi polloi* grew weary
And sat upon the floor
And told each other stories
Until the clock struck four.
They drew each other pictures
One person sang a song
But was careful at the end
To say 'Of course *they* won't be long'.

The artists and the poets
And the people who write books
The musicians and the journalists
And the Nouvelle Cuisine cooks
Sent word they couldn't make it
They couldn't leave the town.
They were meeting V I P's for drinks
And couldn't make it down.

The gherkins went untasted
The crisps were never crunched
The Chablis kept its cork in
The Twiglets went unmunched
But still the people waited
For a hundred million days
And just to help to pass the time
They wrote and acted plays.

They carved a pretty pattern
On the panel of the door.
They painted lovely pictures on the
Coldly concrete floor
They sang in pretty harmony
About the epic wait.
Then hush! . . . Was that a car we heard
Was that a creaking gate?

It's the sculptors on the gravel
It's the poets wild-eyed
Quick open wide the door to
Let the journalists inside.
Oh welcome to our party!
We thought you'd never come
So sad we ate the food though
We haven't left a crumb!

For in the time of waiting
The *hoi polloi* grew brave
They went into the room
And took the things they craved.
And the poets and the sculptors
And the artists and the cooks
And the women good at music
And the men who wrote the books
And the journalists and actors
And the people trained to sing
Stood waiting ever after for the party to begin.

A Mole in Moscow

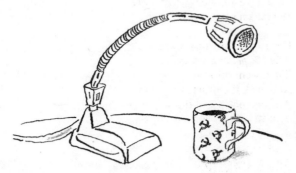

September 1985

Woke up at 6am in the morning. Got out of bed carefully because the dog was spread-eagled across my bed, flat on its back, with its legs in the air. At first I thought it was dead, but I checked its pulse and found signs of life, so I just slid out from underneath its warm fur. The dog's dead old now and needs its sleep.

After measuring my chest and shoulders I had a thorough wash in cold water. I read somewhere (I think it was one of Mr Paul Johnson's articles) that 'cold water makes a man of you'. I've been a bit worried about my maleness lately, somewhere along the line I seem to have picked up too many female hormones.

I've been to see the doctor about it, but as usual he was most unsympathetic. I asked if I could have some of my female hormones taken out. Dr Grey laughed a horrible, bitter laugh and gave his usual advice, which was to go out and have my head kicked about in a rugby scrum. As I was leaving his surgery he said 'And I don't want to see you back here for at least two months'. I asked, 'Even if I'm taken seriously ill?' He muttered,

'*Especially* if you're taken seriously ill'. I'm considering reporting him to his superiors; all this worry has affected my poetry output. I used to be able to turn out at least four poems an hour, but now I'm down to three a week. If I'm not careful I'll dry up altogether.

In my desperation I went to the Lake District on the train. I was struck down by the beauty of the place, although saddened to find that there were no daffodils flashing in my outer eye as in William Wordsworth the old Lake poet. I asked an ancient country yokel why there were no daffodils about. He said, 'It's July, lad'. I repeated loudly and clearly, (because he was obviously a halfwit) 'Yes I know that, but why are there no *daffodils* about?' 'It's July,' he roared. At that point I left the poor deranged soul. It's sad that nothing can be done for such pathetic geriatric cases. I blame the government. Since they put rat poison in the water supply most of the adult population have gone barmy.

I sat on a rock that Wordsworth once sat on and thrilled to think that where my denim was now was where his moleskin used to be. A yob had scrawled on the rock, 'What's wiv this Wordsworth?' Another, more cultivated hand, had written underneath: 'You mindless vandal, how dare you bespoil this precious rock which has been here for millions of years. If you were here I'd flog you to within an inch of your life. Signed, A. Geologist'. Somebody else had written underneath, 'Flog *me* instead. Signed, A. Masochist'. After eating my tuna-fish sandwiches and drinking my low calorie orange drink, I walked around the lake trying to feel inspired, but by tea-time nothing had happened so I put my pen and exercise book back into my carrier-bag and hurried back to the station to catch the train back to the Midlands.

It was just my luck to have to share a compartment with hyperactive two-year-old twins and their worn-out mother. When the twins weren't having spectacular tantrums on the floor they were both standing six inches away from me, *staring* at me with unblinking evil eyes. It used to be my ambition to have a farmhouse full of Hovis-like children. I would imagine looking out of my study window to see them all frolicking amongst the combine harvesters. With Pandora, their mother, saying; 'Shush! . . . Daddy is working', whereupon the children would blow me kisses with their podgy fingers and run into the stone-flagged kitchen to eat the cakes that Pandora had just taken from the oven. However since my experience with the mad twins I have decided *not* to spread my seed. Indeed I may ask my parents if I can have a vasectomy for my eighteenth birthday.

When I got home I hurried round to Pandora's house to tell her about this change in my future plans. Pandora said, *'Au contraire, chéri*, should we still be having a long term relationship. I should like to have one child when I am forty-six years of age. The child will be a girl. She will be beautiful and immensely gifted. Her name will be Liberty.' I said, 'But do women's reproductive organs still reproduce at the age of forty-six?' Pandora said, *'Mais naturellement, chéri*, and anyway there is always the test tube option'.

Mr Braithwaite came into the room and said, 'Pandora, make your mind up. Are you going to Russia or are you not?' Pandora said, 'Not. I can't leave the cat.' They then had a furious row. I could hardly believe my ears. Pandora was turning down a week in Russia with her father just because her stinking old moggy was about to give birth for the fourth time! During a pause in the argument I said, 'I would give my right leg to go to the country of Dostoyevsky's birth'.

However Mr Braithwaite didn't respond with an invitation for me to accompany him. How mean can you get? The Co-op Dairy had given him two tickets to go on a fact-finding tour of milk distribution in Moscow. (Mrs Braithwaite had refused to go because she'd recently joined the SDP.) So a ticket was going spare. Yet the tight git was denying me the glorious opportunity of studying revolution in the raw. When Mr Braithwaite had gone into the garden to savagely mow the lawn Pandora said, 'You *shall* go to Russia'. She worked on her father for a whole week. She refused to eat, she played her stereo system at full decibels. She invited her 'Hell's Angels' friends for tea every day. Her punk friends came to supper and I had breakfast with the family most mornings. By the end of the week Mr Braithwaite was a broken man and Mrs Braithwaite was begging him to take me behind the Iron Curtain. Eventually, after Pandora held an open air reggae concert on the back lawn, Mr Braithwaite relented.

He came to our house at 11 o'clock one Sunday morning, so I got my parents out of bed and we had a meeting at our kitchen table. They enthusiastically agreed to me going to Russia for a week. My mother said, 'Great, George, we could have a second honeymoon while Adrian's away!' My father said, 'Yeah, mum'll look after the baby. We can rediscover ourselves, eh, Pauline?' They slopped over each other for a bit and then turned their attention back to the proceedings for, knowing that I was a virgin traveller, Mr Braithwaite had brought a passport form with him and I filled it in carefully under his supervision. I only made one mistake. Where it said 'sex' I put 'not yet', instead of putting 'male'.

We turned the house upside down looking for my birth certificate before my mother remembered that it was framed and hanging on Grandma's front room wall. My father was sent round to fetch it while Mr Braithwaite took me to have my passport photographs taken in a slot machine. On the way, in the car, I practised facial expressions. I wanted my photographs to show the *real* Adrian Mole. Warm and clever, yet enigmatic and with just a hint of sensuousness. In the event, the photographs were disappointing. I looked like a spotty youth with just a hint of derangement in my sticking-out eyes. After everyone, apart from me, had had a good laugh at the photographs my mother reluctantly wrote a cheque out for fifteen pounds and then the documents were checked and double-checked by Mr Braithwaite before being put into a large envelope. While he did this I examined him carefully, for he was to be my travelling companion and room mate for a week. Would I be able to stand the shame of being seen in the company of a man wearing flared trousers and a paisley patterned waistcoat? Too late! The die was cast! Fate had thrown us together!

As he left, clutching my documentation, he said: 'Adrian, during the week we are in Moscow do you promise, swear, give me your word, that you will not utter *one* word about the Norwegian leather industry?' Astonished I said, 'Of course. If, for some reason, you find my mini-lectures on the Norwegian leather industry *offensive*, then of course I won't mention it'. Mr Braithwaite said, 'Oh I don't find your constant monologues on the Norwegian leather industry *offensive*, just deeply, deeply boring'. Then he got into his car and went to put the documents through the door of the Passport Office.

If this was a film, then leaves would blow across the screen and pages of diaries would riffle, trains would roar and calendars would have months torn from them by unseen hands. But as this is just me speaking then all I need to tell you is that time went by, and I got my passport and my visa by second-class post. In the days before I left England for Russia I also got advice. My Grandma said, 'If the Russians offer to show you the salt mines refuse and ask to be shown a shoe factory instead'. My mother advised me *not* to mention that at the age of fourteen she had been thrown out of the Young Communist League (Norwich Branch) for fraternising with American soldiers. Pandora advised against buying her a light amber necklace saying she preferred the *dark* amber, and Mr O'Leary from over the road advised me not to go at all. He said. 'The Russians are godless heathens, Adrian'. Mrs O'Leary said, 'Yes, and so are you, Declan, you haven't been to Mass for over two years'.

The worst part of the journey to Russia was the M1 motorway. Mr Braithwaite's Volvo was almost sucked under the passing lorries several times. In fact at Watford Gap Mr Braithwaite lost his nerve and the capable hands of Mrs Braithwaite took the wheel. It was the first time I had flown in a plane so I was expecting sympathy and a bit of cherishing from the airstewardesses who stood by the plane door. I said: 'This is the first time I've flown, I may need extra attention during the flight'. The woman said in broken English, 'Well you won't get it from me, Englishman, I will be too busy flying the plane'. Mr Braithwaite went pale when I told him that the pilot was a woman. Then he remembered that he was an avowed feminist and said, 'Jolly good'. Apart from my putting my seat belt around my neck, the flight was uneventful. The passengers concentrated on hiding or eating the garlic sausage and cream crackers they were served for lunch; but they warmed up a bit when the vodka came round, and by the time we landed at the airport just outside Moscow some of them were disgustingly drunk and were not good examples of Western Capitalist Society.

The airport was ill-lit and a bit chaotic, especially when it came to collecting luggage. Nearly everybody had brought Marks and Spencers luggage so quite a few arguments ensued and suitcases had to be opened on the floor, and underwear examined before the rightful owners managed to sort out the 'Y' fronts from the silk culottes.

A big blonde woman stood in a gloomy corner of the arrival

lounge, holding a placard saying 'Intourist'. Five hundred people milled around her asking her questions.

Mr Braithwaite was bleating, 'I'm here to study milk distribution; my name is Ivan Braithwaite; am I in the right place?' The big blonde woman threw her placard down, clapped her hands and yelled 'All you foreigners are to be quiet. I am thinking I am in Moscow Zoo. Now you are to sit on your suitcases and wait.'

We waited and waited, more light bulbs went out and then in the gathering gloom four people arrived holding placards. One said, 'Siberia', one said 'Moscow'. Another one said 'Milk'. Mr Braithwaite and I stood by the 'Milk' placard and were eventually joined by two German dairy farmers, three retired English milkmen and a dyslexic American family who thought the sign said 'Minsk'. We were invited aboard a coach and our guide gave us a commentary on the Moscow suburbs we were passing through. The dyslexic American daughter peered out of the window and said, 'Gross . . . where's the shops for chrissake?' Her mother said, 'Honey we're in the suburbs, the shops are downtown'. No shops could be seen, although one of the English ex-Milkmen spotted a dairy and applauded, which made our guide smile for the first time.

The hotel we stopped in was monolithic and swarming with every nationality on earth. Our guide screamed above the babble of languages, 'Be patient please while I am wrestling with your room keys. If I am lost forever you musk ask for Rosa. It is not my name but it will do. My name in Russian is too difficult for your clumsy tongues'. I fell asleep on the marble floor and woke hours later to the sound of a heavy metal key jangling in my ear.

Having checked the room for hidden microphones, I got into bed in my underwear because my grandma had warned me that secret television cameras were behind every mirror and I did not like the thought of my English genitals being mocked by unseen viewers. Mr Braithwaite fell instantly asleep in the bed next to me but I lay awake for hours listening to the trams outside the hotel and composing a poem in my head:

OH MOSCOW TRAMS

Are your wheels revolutionary?
Are your carriages forged from the steel
of conflict?

Are there bloodstains on the uncut moquette
of your seats?
Do your passengers keep to the tracks of
sacrifice and denial?
I, Adrian Mole will soon know
For in the morning I will be a fellow traveller.

In the morning Mr Braithwaite was nowhere to be seen. My first thought was of abduction, but then I found a note on the toilet seat, it said 'Enjoy your day, see you late tonight'. So, I was alone in Moscow. I put a towel over the bathroom mirror before attending to my toilette. Then, dressed in my best, I went down in the lift to breakfast. The dining room was like an aircraft hangar and was full of Communists eating black bread and drinking coffee. I sat next to a very dark man in robes who was in Moscow to buy gear-levers for his tractor factory in Africa. We chatted for a while but we had little in common, so I turned to my neighbour who turned out to be a Norwegian . . . what a stroke of luck! I spoke at great length about the Norwegian leather industry but instead of being interested he got up and left abruptly, leaving his breakfast half eaten. What a strange moody race are the Scandinavians!

Rosa stomped into the dining room and ordered her party to get on a coach. The American family, the three milkmen, the two German farmers and me were taken to see the sights. We had ten minutes at the Kremlin during which the American girl sold her camera, boots and umbrella to a disaffected whining youth who complained about his country, until Rosa hit him round the head and said, 'No other country would let you in anyway. You are a disgraceful *pretty crook*.' I think she must have meant *petty crook* because the youth was very unattractive. Then we got back into the coach and went to see the Bolshoi Theatre and the Olympic Stadium and the residence of the British Ambassador and museums galore until it was time for lunch.

The milkmen, Arthur, Arnold and Harry reeled across the foyer and complained that they hadn't visited any dairies. They had been drinking and it wasn't milk. Vodka I suspect. Rosa was involved in a bitter argument with the American family who wanted to know when they would be leaving for Minsk, so she didn't listen to the milkmen's wild ramblings.

For lunch I joined a table of old aristocratic Englishwomen who were moaning that, for some inexplicable reason, they had spent the day touring Milk Distribution Centres. A deputation of them approached Rosa pleading to be taken to the Ballet.

The afternoon was free so I went for a walk in Gorky Park and looked for bodies. Loads of Russians were there walking about like English people do. Some were licking ice-creams, some were talking and laughing and some were sunbathing in their underwear with rouble notes on their noses to prevent sunburn. Indeed such was the heat that I was forced to go back to the hotel and take off my balaclava, mother's fur hat, mittens, big overcoat, four sweaters, shirt and two T-shirts.

In the evening we were coached off to the Opera where I and most of the Russians in the audience fell asleep, and the American girl sold her Sony headset. Mr Braithwaite came back very late and very drunk. Vodka doesn't smell but I *knew*. He got into bed without a word and snored very loudly. By now I was convinced he was a spy. The pattern continued throughout our three days in Moscow. I would wake up, find a note from Mr Braithwaite and so would be forced to throw myself on the mercy of 'Intourist'. By this time I was boggle-eyed with culture and longed for a bit of English apathy and gross materialism.

So, on my last afternoon in Moscow I did a brave thing. I went down into the bowels of the chandeliered metro in an attempt to find Moscow's shopping centre. I put a five kopek coin in a machine, got my ticket and descended into splendours of marble and gilt. Trains arrived every three minutes and took me and crowds of Russian people speeding along towards the shops. I attracted a few curious glances (spotty complexions are rare in Russia); but most people were reading heavy intellectual books with funny writing on them or learning piano concertos by Tchaikovsky.

I got out OK, found the shops and four hours later was returning to the hotel with a giant Russian doll which contained thirty other shrinking dolls inside it. Just like in *Tinker, Tailor* on TV. Pandora will get the biggest doll, and my father will get the smallest. As I entered the hotel lobby I saw Mr Braithwaite sitting on a sofa with a voluptuous Russian woman wearing a lime-green trouser suit and platform shoes. She was toying erotically with the flares of Mr Braithwaite's trousers, and I saw him catch her hand and lick the palm. God! It was a revolting sight! I felt like shouting 'Mr Braithwaite, pull yourself together, you're an Englishman'. When they saw me coming they sprang apart. She was introduced as Lara, an expert on the diseases of cow's udders.

I smiled coldly, then left them together, unable to witness the naked lust in their middle-aged eyes. Three roubles were burning a hole in my sock, so I removed my shoe, took the money out and summoned a taxi. 'Take me to Dostoyevsky's grave,' I cried. The taxi driver said: 'How much money do you have?' 'Three roubles' I replied. 'It ain't enough, sunshine' he said, 'Dostoyevsky's grave is in Leningrad'. I complimented him on his English and slunk back into the hotel, did my packing and prepared to fly back.

Lara was at the airport. She gave Mr Braithwaite a single carnation. There was a lot of palm licking and sighing and talk about their 'souls'. Mr Braithwaite gave Lara a copy of *The Dairy Farmer's Weekly*, two pairs of Marks & Spencers socks, a toilet roll and a packet of 'Bic' razors. She wept pitifully.

Mrs Braithwaite and Pandora were waiting beyond the barrier at Gatwick. As we walked towards them Mr Braithwaite sighed in a deep Russian Chekhovian way and said, 'Adrian, Mrs Braithwaite may not understand about Lara'. I said 'Mr Braithwaite, I do not understand about Lara myself. How *anyone* could have an affair with a woman wearing a lime-green trouser suit and platform shoes is beyond me'. This speech took me though the barrier and into the arms of Pandora and England. Oh, Leicester! Leicester! Leicester!

Mole on Lifestyle

I often look back on my callow youth, and when I do a smile flits across my now mature but pitted face. I hardly recognize the naïve boy I once was. To think that I once believed that Evelyn Waugh was a woman! Of course now, with a couple of 'O' levels under my belt, I am far more sophisticated and I know that Evelyn Waugh, should he be alive today, would be very, indeed, *dead* proud of his daughter, Auberon; because of course Evelyn is the *father* of Auberon and not as I once thought, the mother.

I occasionally glance through my early diaries and mourn for my lost innocence, for at the age of thirteen and three quarters, I thought it was sufficient to just have a *life*. I honestly didn't know then that you *can't* just have a life. You have to have a *lifestyle*. So my talk today is about 'Lifestyle', with particular reference to my own.

I will take you through a typical day. I will introduce you to my friends and family. I will refer fleetingly to my diet, toilet habits and my style of dress. My tastes in Art and Literature will be dwelt upon. At the end of my talk perhaps you will have an overview of my lifestyle. Incidentally, and by the way, 'overview' is just one of the thousands of words in my vocabulary, and with a bit of luck I will introduce other uncommon words to you, the listening masses. For I am solely aware of my duty via Radio Four to *educate* and entertain the great British public. For how else are they to rise up and take power if they don't understand the words of power? Or the power of words?

I have been told by my contemporaries that I am quite a trendsetter, although Pandora, the love of my life, maintains that *trendsetter* is a word only used by crumblies and people with one foot in the crematorium.

For instance my style of dress is idiosyncratic. Indeed it is personal to myself. Since radio is not television I will describe what I am wearing at the moment. I will start at the head and work down, to save any confusion. On my head I am wearing a balaclava helmet knitted by my ancient yet nimble-fingered Grandma. I am wearing the balaclava because my Father refuses to switch the central heating on until November 1st every year. He cares not that English summer does not exist anymore. As usual he is being selfish and thinking about paying the boring gas bill.

We move down. Around my neck is a silken cravat which was formerly owned by my dead Grandfather. It is a lucky cravat. My grandfather wore it at Epsom and won half-a-crown on a horse (whatever half-a-crown is). My shirt is proudly, indeed un-ashamedly, from a CND rummage sale. It once belonged to a Canadian lumberjack who had a sweat or, more politely, a perspiration problem, at least so my mother maintains. The smell doesn't bother me as I am used to it, although other people have complained. Under the shirt I wear an 'I love Cliff Richard' T-shirt. A reminder of when I was young and stupid. I *never* unbutton the Canadian shirt. My legs are clad in a pair of executive striped trousers bought at the closing down sale at Woolworths. On my feet are designer training shoes given to me by my best friend Nigel. Poor Nigel suffers from an obsession; he compulsively buys training shoes. The reasons are manifold:

a: He has to be the first in our small town to have the latest style.

b: Because of his inner rage Nigel is always yanking on laces too hard so that they break. He then passes the shoes on to me, claiming he can't be bothered to re-thread the new laces. My own impoverished family benefit from Nigel's impetuousness. We are all walking around in Nigel's new old shoes. Even Grandma is wearing a pair. They are too big for her but, with the wisdom of the old, she found a way of making them fit by stuffing the toes with toilet paper.

Under my training shoes I am wearing a pair of odd socks. One sock is white, one sock is black. No, think not that I am an absent-minded genius who doesn't notice what he puts on his feet. Perhaps I am a genius, but not an absent-minded one. No, my choice of hosiery is completely calculated. Indeed it is symbolic. The white socks stands for my inner purity and morality: for I am against violence and Polaris missiles and cruelty to battery hens. The black sock stands for the evil in my soul, such as wanting to go the whole hog with Pandora and fantasising about blowing up tower blocks (minus suicidal tenants of course).

Thus I am a walking dichotomy. On my feet I carry the problems of the world. Naturally the *hoi-polloi* do not recognise this salient fact. They cry out 'Eh ... yer wearin' odd socks!' To these crude rejoinders I simply reply, in my modulated tones, 'No, 'tis you who is wearing the odd socks, my friend.' Some of them walk away marvelling, although some of them, to be quite honest, don't.

As to personal adornments. I am wearing a gold-plated chain and locket. In the locket are the remains of a dried up autumn leaf. The leaf represents the frailty of the human condition. It was given to me by Pandora in a moment of autumnal ardour. Round my left wrist I wear a copper bangle which hopefully will guard against me contracting arthritis in old age. On my right wrist I wear a plastic waterproof watch which will allow me, should I feel the need, to dive to a depth of a hundred feet.

I have one other personal adornment that nobody knows about apart from me and one other person. It is a tiny tattoo secreted in a private part of my body. The tattoo says 'Mum and Dad' and dates from a time of their marital instability. I now regret my impetuosity because this tattoo will prevent me from partaking in nude sunbathing in the years to come. So, when I am a poet millionaire and I am lying on my personal Greek island I will be the only person amongst my guests to be wearing trunks.

However, the Greek Island home is for the future. My present domestic abode is a semi-detached house in a suburban cul-de-sac in the Midlands. Yes, like many of my fellow Britons, I live with a party wall between me and another family's intimate secrets. I will never understand why it is called a 'party' wall because *when* our next door neighbours throw a party every celebratory sound is heard. Tonic bottles unscrewed, cherries dropping into cocktails, women making brittle conversation, men being sick. So, if the purpose of a party wall is to prevent party noise from spilling into the house adjoining then I have this to say to the builders of Britain, 'You have failed, Sirs'. Now I will take you through one of my typical days.

The dog usually wakes me up at 7 o'clock or thereabouts. It is dead old now and has a weak bladder. I get out of bed, and in my underpants and vest I open the back door and let it out to cock its leg on our next door neighbour's lawn. I make myself a cup of coffee and take it back to bed with me while I read an edifying work of literature. At the moment I am reading *Wittgenstein Primer* written by T. Lowes MA. Trin. Dub. Sometimes for amusement I may turn to something less intellectually straining; *Wings On My Suitcase: personal adventures of an air hostess* introduced and edited by Gerard Tikell, is a good example. Then again, even reminiscences of air hostesses may prove to be too demanding at such an early hour. So for even lighter relief I will turn to my old *Beano* annuals.

I have a baby sister now and she usually climbs out of her cot at 7.30 dragging her wet nappy with her. She barges into my room and gabbles some childish gibberish to which I respond curtly, 'Go and wake Mummy and Daddy up, Rosemary'. I refuse to bastardise her name and call her 'Rosie'. She staggers out on her wobbly legs and beats her tiny fists on my parent's door. Muffled curses tell me that my parents are awake, so I quickly get out of bed and run into the bathroom before anyone else. I lie in my bath and ignore rattlings on the door and demands for entry. I insist on a period of quiet before I start my day. Anyway it's not my fault that the only lavatory is placed in the bathroom, is it? I've lost track of the times I've told my father to install a downstairs lavatory. After completing a meticulous toilette, topped off with liberal lashings of my father's after-shave mixed with my mother's Yardley water, I emerge from the bathroom, have a row with my parents, who are standing cross-legged outside the door, and go and go down to breakfast. I warm myself a frozen croissant and make a cup of Earl Grey Tea *sans* milk and sit down to study the world news. We take the *Guardian* and the *Sun* so I am quite an expert on the latest developments concerning 'whale conservation' and also the mammary development of Miss Samantha Fox. My parents are victims of Thatcherism so neither of them is working, which means they are able to hang about and linger over their breakfasts. Rosemary is a disgusting eater. I always leave the table before she starts on her porridge.

I go to my room, collect my books and study aids and go to college. I ignore most of my fellow students, who are usually thronging the corridors laughing about the previous night's drunken debauch. Instead I make my way to a classroom and quietly study before the lessons begin. For, while I am an intellectual (indeed almost a genius), at the same time I am not very clever and so need to study harder than anyone else.

I spend each break with Pandora. We usually talk about world events. Pandora only wears black clothes as she is in mourning for the world. This has led to her being called 'Barmy Braithwaite' by unthinking morons amongst the student body and also, I regret to report, some of the academic staff. We usually walk home together and on the way call in to see Bert Baxter who is now the oldest man on the electoral roll. Pandora takes Sabre the alsatian for an angry prowl around the recreation ground, while I clean Bert up and listen to his incoherent ramblings about Lenin and the 'needs of the Proletariat to rise up'. (Bert refuses to die until he sees the fall of Capitalism so it looks as though Bert will be with us for quite a while yet, unfortunately.) When Bert and Sabre have been pacified and fed and watered, Pandora and I walk home together. We part at the entrance to my cul-de-sac and she strolls off to her tree-lined avenue and her detached, book-lined house and I go to my previously described more horrible domestic living unit.

The warm scent of home baking does not greet me as I enter the kitchen. So I create my own smell by baking scones. Here is my recipe but remember before you rush for pencil and paper that the recipe is copyright and owned by me, Adrian Mole. So, should you wish to bake scones to this recipe then you will need to send money to me.

A. MOLE'S SCONES

Ingredients
4 oz flour or metric equivalent
2 oz butter or metric equivalent
2 oz sugar or metric equivalent
1 egg (eggs are still only eggs)

Method
Beat up all the ingredients. Make a tin greasy, throw it all
in. Turn oven to number 5. Wait until scones are higher
than they were. Should be 12 minutes, but keep opening
oven door every 30 seconds.

So, crunching, on my fresh-from-the-oven scones, I wind down
from my day. At this time I may give Rosemary a few moments
attention. Last night I built the GPO Tower from her lego
bricks, but while my back was turned Rosemary smashed it to
pieces, and then had the nerve to laugh amongst the rubble. This
is typical of her behaviour. I am sure she is going to grow up to
be psychotic. She is already quite unmanageable. She empties
drawers, switches the television knobs on and off, throws her soft
toys down the lavatory pan and flies into a rage if she is restrained
in any way. I have urged my parents to take her to the Child
Guidance Clinic before it is too late, but my mother defends her
saying, 'Rosie is quite normal, Adrian, all toddlers behave like
Attila the Hun. Why do you think so many mothers are on
tranquillisers?' In the early evening I make a point of watching a
soap opera or two. I think it is very important for us intellectuals
to keep in touch with popular culture. We cannot live in ivory
towers, unless of course the ivory towers have a television aerial
on the roof.

My parents are trying to save their marriage by playing bad-
minton together on alternative Wednesdays. Otherwise, apart from
this fortnightly outing, they clutter the house up in the evenings
so I am forced to keep in my room or take to the streets. I honestly
can't understand how they can bear each other's company. Their
conversation consists of moaning about money and whining about
wages – the wages they haven't got.

I make few demands on them. All I require is a jar of multi-
vitamins once a week plus clean linen and courtesy. However I

wouldn't like you to switch off thinking that I'm not fond of my parents. In my own way I'm very close to them. It's hard not to be. We live in a small house. They do have their good points. My father is quite a wit after a couple of glasses of vodka, and my mother is known for her compassion towards other married women. In fact she is in the middle of organising a local group of them. I read somewhere that it is important for families to have bodily contact, so I make a point of patting my parents' shoulders as I pass by. It costs nothing and seems to please them. However at 8 o'clock, when the lounge is full of cigarette smoke, I make my excuses and leave for the outside world.

I sometimes meet up with Barry Kent and we chat about which of his friends is in court, and who's in borstal. Occasionally we discuss Barry's poetry; he was taught to read and write during his last period in a detention centre. It was a progressive place that had a poet in residence so instead of breaking rocks Barry was forced to split infinitives and then put them together again. Some of his stuff is quite good, primitive of course, but then Barry is practically a certified moron so it is only to be expected. Still, at least he's making a living out of his poetry. In the guise of 'Baz the Skinhead Poet' he tours pubs and rock venues, and shouts poetry at the audience. Sometimes they shout back and then there's a fight. Barry always wins.

On my way home I call in to see Pandora who is usually sitting under the anglepoise lamp bent over 'A' level homework. On the wall above her desk are two notices written in pink neon marker pen. One says, 'GET TO OXFORD OR DIE' the other says 'GO TO CAMBRIDGE AND LIVE'. There are five exclamation marks after each of them. We share a cup of cocoa, or if her parents are out, gin and tonic. Then we kiss passionately for about five minutes, longer if it's a gin night, and I make my way home racked with latent sexuality. On such occasions I am pleased to find it's raining. There's nothhing like a cold shower to ease sexual frustration.

By 11 o'clock I am in bed with the dog, reading, with a digestive biscuit and a cup of cocoa on my bedside table. It isn't the lifestyle I would choose for myself. Given the choice I would opt for a mixture of Prince Andrew and Prince Edward's social life, Ted Hughes's working life and the Wham or Mick Jagger's romantic life. But at least I've *got* a life. Some people haven't.

And I'm on the verge, the very kerb of the dual carriageway of Fate. Will I go one way towards London, celebrity and media attention? . . . Or will I go the other way, towards the provinces, and be forced to write letters to the local paper in order to see my name in print? A third possibility occurs to me. I could break down at a roundabout and remain, unsung, in limbo.

But I mustn't burden you, kind listener, with my introspective musings. And anyway I shall have to finish now − it's started raining and my jeans are on the line.

Mole's Prizewinning Essay

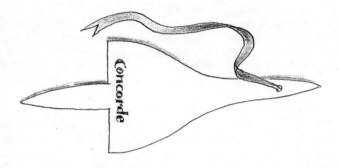

MONDAY

Oh joy! . . . Oh rapture! . . . At last I have made my mark on the world of literature. My essay entitled 'A Day in the Life of an Air Stewardess' has won second prize in the British Airways Creative Writing Competition.

My prizes are: A Concorde-shaped bookmark inscribed in gold leaf by Melvyn Bragg, a hostess apron which has been donated by 'The Society for Distressed Air Stewardesses', and £50.

Here, for posterity, is my prizewinning essay.

A DAY IN THE LIFE OF AN AIR STEWARDESS
BY A. MOLE

Jonquil Storme opened her languorous blue eyes and looked at the clock. 'Oh drat and bother', she expectorated. The clock said seven o'clock and Jonquil was due at Heathrow Airport at seven fifteen, where she was in charge of Concorde.

Jonquil stretched out her lissome white hand and picked up the phone. Her other hand dialled the number: with her other hand she fondled an orchid that stood next to her bed in a jam jar.

'Hi, Brett!' she said into the receiver . . . 'Jonquil here, darling. I'm late, our night of passion wore me out and caused me to oversleep.' Brett's manly chuckle reverberated down the phone.

'OK Jonquil', he guffawed, 'I'll tell the passengers that there is snow on the runway. Take your time my darling!'

Jonquil put the phone down and sank into the pillows that were still impregnated with Brett's hair oil. She wondered if she would ever get to marry Brett, the Captain of Concorde, and whether the excuse about snow on the runway would be believed. After all it was *July*. Thus ruminating, Jonquil showered in the shower and dressed in the dressing room. Soon she was soignée and was climbing into her Maserati open-topped sports car to the gapes of ordinary dingy passers by.

Soon she was wriggling up the steps of Concorde in her high heeled shoes. Brett met her at the door of the plane and gave her a French kiss. The passengers didn't mind at all, in fact they applauded and cheered. A jolly American shouted 'God bless you, Captain!'

Brett flashed his manly teeth and went to the front of the plane and switched the engine on. Jonquil went round smiling at the passengers and opening jars of caviar. Soon the champagne corks were popping and the passengers were lying about in stupours. The flight was smooth and without hazards and when Concorde reached New York Brett asked Jonquil to be his bride. So, after having blood tests for diseases, Brett and Jonquil were married in the elevator of the Empire State Building. Soon it was time to turn Concorde round and go home to London. Jonquil was dead proud of her new gold ring and Brett flew the plane better than he ever had before.

As Jonquil got into bed that night she said to herself, 'What a lucky girl I am. To think I almost became a Domestic Science teacher'. She looked at Brett's matted black hair on the Laura Ashley pillow and smiled. It had been the most exciting day of her life.

THE END (Copyright World Wide owned by A. Mole)

The Sarah Ferguson Affair

Thursday July 17th

I'm sick of reading about how handome Prince Andrew is. To me he looks like the morons studying bricklaying and plastering at college, there is something about his neck that cries out for a hod of bricks. And those big white ruthless teeth! It makes me shudder to think of them nibbling at Fergie's defenceless neck. So some women like tall, well-built men who can fly helicopters and have gob-smacking bank accounts and Coutts gold cards. But personally I think Fergie is throwing herself away on him.

Miss Sarah Ferguson was born to be the wife of Adrian Mole. I have written to tell her so, and to implore her to change her mind before 23rd July. As yet I have received no reply. She must be agonising over her decision: 'Riches, glamour and publicity with Prince Andrew, or poverty, introspection and listening to poetry with Adrian Mole' – not an easy choice.

Sarah Ferguson, oh Sarah Ferguson,
Your name is on my lips constantly.
Don't marry Andy, his legs are bandy.
Come to Leicester, come to Leicester, marry me!
Leave the palace, grab a taxi,
I'll be waiting at the end of the M1.
We'll go to my house, meet my parents,
I know the dog and you will get along.

Friday July 18th

No letter from Sarah Ferguson today.

I have rung Buckingham Palace but the (no doubt powdered and bewigged) flunkey refused to let me speak to her. He said, 'Miss Ferguson is taking no calls from strangers.' I said, 'Listen, my man, I am no *stranger* to Miss Ferguson, she is my soul mate.' I'm not sure but I could have sworn the flunky muttered, 'Arsehole mate,' before he slammed the phone down. There is nothing else to do but go to Buckingham Palace and tackle her face to face.

I have sent a Telemessage to my ginger-haired love:
Sarah, I am coming to you. Meet me at the Palace gate at high noon.
    Yours with unvanquished love,
        Adrian Mole (18¼).
P.S. I will be wearing sunglasses, and carrying a Marks and Spencer carrier-bag.

Saturday   July 19th
BUCKINGHAM PALACE, 1.30PM.

She did not come. I asked a mounted policeman if Sarah was at home. He said, 'Yes, she's inside having waving lessons from the Queen Mother.' I asked him if he would deliver a note to her from me, but he got distracted by a coach-load of excitable Japanese tourists who were measuring his horse and taking down its specifications. No doubt they are going to copy it and flood the world with cheap police horses. Will we English never learn?

I made my way home to the dreary provinces by train. An old fat woman kept up a non-stop monologue about her plans for the royal wedding day. I wanted to cry out, 'You old fat fool, you will be watching an empty screen on the 23rd because *there will be no royal wedding.* So cancel your order for two dozen crusty cobs and a crate of assorted bottles of pop.' I *wanted* to cry these words out but, of course, I didn't; people would have thought I was a teenage lunatic obsessed with Sarah Ferguson, whereas of course I am anything but.

Sunday   July 20th

Sarah has not replied to my letter yet.
  Perhaps she has run out of stamps.

Monday   July 21st

I asked the postman if there was anything for me from Buckingham Palace. He replied, 'Ho, has Ted Hughes croaked it? H'are you the next Poet Laureate? H'if you hare, may I h'offer my h'utmost congratulations?'
  No wonder England's going to the dogs with public servants of his calibre.

7pm. Pandora Braithwaite rang from Leningrad tonight.
  I asked her how she was getting on with her Russian lessons. She said, 'Oh, amazingly well, I joined in a most stimulating debate in the turnip queue this morning. Workers and intellectuals discussed the underlying symbolism of *The Cherry Orchard.* I ventured the opinion, in Russian of course, that the cherries represented the patriarchal balls of Mother Russia, thus proving that Chekhov was A C/D C.'
  I asked how the assembled geniuses in the turnip queue had reacted to her analysis. Pandora said, 'Oh, they failed to understand it, bloody peasants!' The line started to go faint, so Pandora shouted, 'Adrian, video-tape the royal wedding for me, darling.' Then the phone went dead, and Pandora was lost to me.

Tuesday   July 22nd

My Sarah was on the front page of the paper this morning, wearing a most indecent low-cut dress. That oaf Andrew was quite openly leering at her cleavage. When Sarah is my wife I shall insist that she wears cardigans buttoned up to the neck.

I'm with the Moslems on this one.

No letter. No hope left, the wedding is tomorrow, I shall not watch it. I shall walk the streets clutching my despair. Oh God! Oh Sarah!

Wednesday   July 23rd

MY SARAH'S WEDDING DAY

Sarah! Sarah! Sarah!

I sobbed into my pillow for so long this morning that the feathers stuck together and formed lumps like bits of dead chickens. Eventually I rose, dressed in black, and made a simple yet nutritious breakfast. My mother came down and through cigarette smoke said, 'What's up with your face?'

I replied quietly, yet with immense dignity, 'I am in the deepest despair, Mother.'

'Why, are your piles playing you up again?' She coughed.

I left the kitchen, shaking my head from side to side in a pitying fashion, whilst at the same time saying, *sotto voce*, 'Lord, have mercy on the philistines I am forced to live with, for they know not what they say.'

My father overheard and said, 'Oh, got bleedin' religion now, has he?'

I passed Grandma on her way to our house. She was carrying a tea-tray piled high with little fancy cakes, iced with the entwined initials 'FA.' Grandma was in her best clothes; her hat swayed with exotic and long extinct birds' feathers, she was wearing net gloves and a fox's claw brooch. She was ecstatically happy. She cried out, 'Hello, Adrian, my little love, have you got a kiss for your Grandma?' I kissed her rouged cheek and walked on before she saw the tears in my eyes. She croaked, 'Happy royal wedding day, Adrian.'

I passed the Co-op where the Union Jack hung upside-down, and the Sikh temple where it was hung correctly. I bought a

commemorative Andy and Fergie mug and blacked Prince
Andrew's big-jawed face out with a black marker pen, then I sat
on the side of the canal, put some flowers in the mug and wrote a
last letter to Sarah:

Dear Princess Sarah,
You will soon tire of the loon you married (he looks like the sort to
hog the bedclothes to me). As soon as you grow even a little weary
of him, remember I am waiting for you here in Leicester. I cannot
promise you riches (although I have £139.37 in the Market
Harborough Building Society) but I can offer intellectual chit-chat
and my body, which is almost unsullied and is years younger than
your husband's.

Well, Sarah, I won't keep you as I expect your husband is
shouting oafishly for your attention.

I remain, Madam,
Your most humble and obedient servant,
Adrian Mole.

The Mole/Kent letters

To:
Barry Kent
ITK SR
Unit 2
Ridley Young Offenders Centre
Ridley-Upon-The-Dour
LINCOLNSHIRE

Leicester
April 2 1987

Dear Baz,
It was good to see you on Tuesday. The prison uniform suits
you. You should wear more blue when you get out. Also Baz,
non-smoking seems to agree with you, your breath was not as
repellent as usual, why not give up for good? I'm sorry I have
to be the bearer of bad news but somebody has to tell you that
your fiancée Cindy is living with Gary Fullbright, the body
builder, remember him? He won the 'Mr Muscle' competition in
1985. Cindy is expecting his baby in four months time. I expect
you have just reeled back with the shock, so I'll give you time
in which to recover.

Baz, Cindy isn't worthy of your love, don't for God's sake
grieve over her. Her fingernails were never clean, and she had

no dress sense at all. I will never forget that black rubber outfit she wore (with scuffed stilletoes and laddered fishnet tights) to your father's funeral. Also, Baz, she had the intellectual capacity of a withered rubber band. I was chatting to her once about Middle Eastern politics and it became clear to me that she thought Mr Arafat was the Arab equivalent of Mr Kipling – a type of foreign biscuit.

Onto other subjects. Nigel sends his regards, he would like to come and see you but doesn't trust himself not to burst into tears at the prison gate. Also he thinks his appearance might startle your fellow prisoners and leave you open to a certain amount of bullying in the dormitory. He is now a bald-headed Buddhist and wears orange robes and orange flip-flops (in all weathers). But, apart from these superficial changes he is still the same old Nigel, although, sadly, he got the sack from the bank: religious persecution is still alive and well in this country, I fear.

Nothing much has happened here; provincial life drags its weary way through the hours and days and months and years. I think it's time I left the library, Baz. The attitude of the general public towards the books they borrow is contemptuous. Yesterday I found a rasher of bacon inside *A Dictionary of Philosophy*. It had obviously been used as a bookmark. Further on, in the same book, I found a note addressed to a milkman:

Dear Milkman

I'd be most terribly grateful if, from now on you would be as kind as to leave one further pint of skimmed milk. That is to say dating from today (Tuesday) I would like you to deliver two pints of skimmed milk per day. I hope you will join me in my happiness at the news that my wife has returned to me. I know how much you and she enjoyed your little early morning doorstep chats. Alas, I fear I do not have my wife's common touch. However, I am fully appreciative of your achievement in delivering our milk in all weather conditions, and if, in the past, I have given the impression of being surly and uncommunicative, I'm sorry. I'm not at my best in the early morning. I am plagued with a recurring nightmare: I am lecturing to a Hall full of students

when half-way through I realise I am naked. Perhaps
you have similar disturbed nights? From what I've
seen of you from my bedroom window, you seem to
be a sensitive person. You have an intelligent mien.

Don't be offended, milkman, but I would guess
that you have had little education, so, why not let us
help you to educate yourself by browsing along our
well stocked bookshelves? You are welcome to borrow
any book – apart from the first editions which need
very careful handling – normally I would suggest that
the ill-educated use the library but our local branch is
staffed by cretins.

Do think about this proposition and communicate
either 'yea' or 'nay' at the bottom of this page.

With warmest regards,
Richard Blythe-Samson (No. 19)

Nay. You owe me 6 weeks money. Milkman.

Well Baz, I'll sign off now. Hope you don't take it too hard
about Cindy, but somebody had to tell you and who better than
your old mate,
Adrian 'Brains' Mole
P.S. It's my birthday today. I am nineteen and God am I
weary of this life.

Unit 2
April 9th 1987

Dear 'Brains'
Cindy as wrote to me and said it is lies about her and Gary
Fullbright and she said she is not in the club she as just put on
some wait because of working in the hot spud shop she swears
on her dogs head that she stills love me and she is weighting
for me. The reeson she as not bin to see me is becars she has
had migraine you have got a nerv to critisize her you should
look in the mirrer sometime at yourself I av herd bad things
about Pandorra that she is havving it off with allsorts including
china men and yugoslavians their is a screw in hear who as got
a son at oxford university he nows pandorra an he says she is a
slagg wye did you tell me that stuff about the milkman it was

drivval I am goinng mad in hear I want to now what is goinng
on with the lads outside did spig get sentensed yet as marvin
got parrole things like that do not bothur writin if you write
drivvel and if you come to see me argain dress up smart I was
ashammd last time and I got greif from the lads after visitting.
I told them you was not all their but I still got greif my cell
mate is a fat slob is name is clifton there is not room to move
when he is standing up I am aksing for a transferr he is the
fart champion of the prison gary fullbright is lookinggg for
you
    stay cool
    Baz

April 18th 1987

Dear Baz
How dare you infer that Pandora is a slag? She mixes with
Chinese, Russians and Yugoslavians because she is taking
Russian, Serbo-Croatian and Chinese at Oxford. She no doubt
entertains them in her rooms until quite late at night, but
believe me Baz she is not engaging in sexual intercourse with
them. I know for a *fact* that Pandora is a virgin. Unlike you
and Cindy, Pandora and I have a completely honest relationship.
If she were no longer a virgin I would be the first to know. I
will make no further comment on the Cindy/Gary situation
apart from saying that I saw them *together* in *Mothercare* buying
a *baby's bath* and two maternity bras, but from now on my lips
are sealed. I'm sorry you are of the opinion that parts of my
last letter were drivel. I thought the note to the milkman would
amuse you and take your mind off your present surroundings. I
don't blame you for being bitter, though. Two years imprisonment
for criminal damage to a privet hedge does seem harsh. I'm
scared to *cough* in the street these days in case I get done under
the new Public Order Act.
    I haven't had a poem from you for ages Baz. I hope you
haven't given up scribbling. You have a rare, muscular sort of
talent which you musn't waste. You once had a lucrative career
as 'Baz, the Skinhead Poet' on the poetry club circuit. Why not
take this opportunity to write a new collection?
    Yours
    Adrian 'Brains' Mole

May 12 1986

Dear Brains
BANGED UP
Ok. I done it
I damaged a hedge
I broke a few twigs
A few leaves fell off
Hedges grow again.

They said it was privet
in court, in evidence.
Me, I didn't know
I was falling, drunk.
I grabbed this green thing
I fell in, got scratched
couldn't get out again.
The hedges owner called 999.
An old bloke he was
If he'd pulled me out I
woulda gone.
Instead the filth come.
'Hello Baz, you've broken
an hedge.
That's criminal damage, vandalism, wanton,
mindless'
Honest, it was a few twigs, a few green
leaves.
It needed cutting,
'I shan't press charges' said the old man.
But it was too late,
the law had started its machinery up.
It couldn't stop.
Not until the prison gate
opened and took me in.
'Criminal damage to an hedge'
I'm a joke in here.
Psychopaths get more respect
the old man, he was in court.
He wasn't happy. He looked at me
in the dock. His face said,

'I'm not happy.'
I gave him a salute one man to
another.
Then I went down.
                    BAZ KENT
                    (The Skinhead Poet)

                                        June 30th 1987
Dear Baz
Its some months since I wrote to you I know but I've been
very busy with my opus, 'Tadpole', which I am hoping to get
published either in *The Literary Review* or *The Leicester
Mercury*, whichever pays the most. 'Tadpole' is the story-in-
rhyme of a tadpole's difficult journey to froghood. It is 10,000
words in length so far and the tadpole in question is still in the
canal squirming about. So, Baz, as a fellow poet, you can see
my problem. All my waking hours – apart from those in the
stinking library where I am forced to earn my living – are
spent writing. I care nothing for food or rest or taking hot
baths. I haven't changed my clothes in months (apart from
socks and underpants); what care I for the outward trappings of
petit bourgeois society?

There have been complaints at work about my appearance:
Mr Nuggett, Deputy Librarian, said yesterday, 'Mole, I am
giving you the afternoon off. Go home, bathe, wash your hair
and change into clean clothes!'

I replied (with dignity), 'Mr Nuggett, would you have spoken
to Byron, Ted Hughes, or Larkin as you've just spoken to me?'
He was dumbfounded. All he could think to say eventually was
'You used the wrong tense as far as Ted Hughes is concerned,
because, unless there has been a tragic accident or a sudden
illness, I believe Mr Hughes to be most vigorously alive.'

What a pedant!

Your poem 'Banged Up' was quite nice. Must stop now,
'The Tadpole' calls.

Hey ho.
    A. Mole

P.S. Cindy has called the baby Carlsburg.

Adrian Mole Leaves Home

Monday   June 13th

I had a good, proper look at myself in the mirror tonight. I've always wanted to look clever, but at the age of twenty years and three months I have to admit that I look like a person who has never even *heard* of Jung or Updike. I went to a party last week and a girl of sixteen felt obliged to tell me who Gertrude Stein was. I tried to cut her off – inform her that I was conversant with Ms Stein, but I started to choke on a cheese and tomato pizza so the opportunity was lost.

So, the mirror showed me myself, as I am. I'm dark but not dark enough to be interesting: no Celtic broodiness. My eyes are grey. My eyelashes are medium length, nothing exciting here. My nose is high-bridged, but it's a Roman centurion's nose, rather than a senator's. My mouth is thin. Not cruel and thin, and it gets a bit sloppy towards the edges. I *have* got a chin, though. No mean achievement considering my pure English genes.

Since I was a callow youth I've spent a fortune on my skin. I've rubbed and applied hundreds of chemicals and lotions onto and into the offending pustulated layer of epidermis, but alas! to no avail. Sharon Botts, my present girl friend, once described my complexion as being like 'one of them bubble sheets what incontinent people use to protect their mattress.'

As can be seen from the above reproduction of Sharon's speech her knowledge of correct English grammar is minimal, therefore I have taken it upon myself to educate her. I am Henry Higgins to her Eliza Dolittle.

She is worth it. Her measurements are 42–30–38. She's a big girl. Unfortunately she measures thirty inches round the tops of her thighs, and fifteen inches round her ankles. But isn't that just like life? The most beautiful and exotic places on earth also attract mosquitoes don't they? Nothing and nobody is perfect, are they? Apart from Madonna, of course.

Anyway, I suggested to Sharon that she would look wonderful in floor length skirts but she said 'Who the bleedin' hell d'you think I am, sodding Queen Victoria?'

Summer will soon be here and I have a recurring nightmare that Sharon decides to buy and *wear* a mini skirt. In my dream she takes my arm and we stroll down the crowded high street. The public stop and stare, guffawing breaks out. A three-year-old child points at Sharon and says, 'Look at the lady's fat legs.' At this point I wake up sweating and with a pounding heart.

You may be wondering why I, Adrian Mole, a provincial intellectual working in a library and Sharon Botts, a provincial dullard working in a laundry are having a relationship. The answer is, sex. I have grown to be rather keen on it and find it difficult to stop doing it now I've started.

Sharon and I were both virgins when we met which is a piece of good fortune too rare to overlook. What with AIDS and herpes rampaging round the world. But sex is where our relationship begins and ends. Sharon is as bored by my conversation as I am by hers, so we go elsewhere for that. She goes to see her mother and five sisters, and I go to see Pandora Braithwaite, who is the true love of my life.

I've loved Pandora since 1980. Two years ago we went our separate ways, Pandora to Oxford to study Russian, Chinese and Serbo-Croat, and me to stamp books in the library in the town where I was born. I chose library work because I wanted to immerse myself in literature. Ha! The library I work in could easily double as the headquarters of the local Philistines Society.

I have never had a literary conversation at work, never. Neither with the staff nor the borrowers of the books.

My days are spent taking books off shelves and putting books back on the shelves. Occasionally I am interrupted by members of the public asking mad questions: 'Is Jackie Collins here?' To this I reply, after first glancing round the library in an exaggerated fashion. 'Highly unlikely, madam. I believe she lives in Hollywood.'

Sometimes my mother visits me at work, although I have given her strict instructions not to do so. My mother cannot modulate her voice. Her laugh could pickle cabbage. Her appearance is striking and now, in her forty-third year, merging on the eccentric. She has no colour sense. She wears espadrilles. Summer and winter. She disobeys the No Smoking signs and enters doors labelled, Private Staff Only.

My father never visits the library. He claims that the sight of so many books make him ill.

Unfortunately, I am still living at home with my parents (and my five-year-old sister Rosie). This *ménage à quatre* co-exists in a sullen atmosphere. Half the time I feel like somebody in a Chekhov play. We've even got a cherry tree in the front garden.

I've tramped the streets looking for my own cheap apartment. I put an advertisement in the local paper.

> Writer requires a room, preferably garret.
> Non-smoker, respectable.
> Clean habits. References supplied.
> Rent no more than £10 a week.

I received three replies: the first from an old lady who offered me rent free accommodation in return for helping her to feed her thirty-seven cats and nine dogs. The second from an anonymous person who wished to 'thoroughly irrigate my colon'. The third from a Mr QZ Diablo.

I went to inspect the room offered by Mr Diablo. As soon as he opened the front door I knew I would not enjoy living in close proximity to him. Beards irritate me at the best of times and Mr Diablo's cascaded down from his chin and came to a straggling end somewhere near to his navel. However I allowed him to lead the way up the swaying staircase. The room was at the top of the house. It was part-furnished, with a bed and a structure resembling an altar. Purple cloaks hung from hooks in the walls. Mr QZ Diablo said, 'Of course I shall need this room on Thursday evenings for our meetings. We finish just after midnight, would that be too inconvenient?'

'I'm afraid it would,' I said. 'I'd prefer to sort of have the place to myself.'

'You *could* join us,' he suggested, helpfully. 'We're a jolly crowd, though cursed with a diabolical public image.'

I stared down at a red stain. It was on a multi-coloured carpet that only a mad man or mad woman could have designed, possibly in a workshop within the high walls of an institution.

'Only animal blood,' said QZ, reassuringly poking the stain with his bare big toe. 'We don't go in for human sacrifice,' he said comfortingly.

I said the words of the timid and cowardly: 'I'll think about it.'

'Yes you must,' said my host. He then led me down the stairs and out to freedom. I didn't want to tramp the streets on Thursday evenings and neither did I want to wear a purple cloak and mutter incantations over an animal sacrifice with a jolly crowd once a week. So I didn't go and live under Mr QZ Diablo's roof. This was last week.

Tonight my mother said, 'Look, when are you leaving home? We want to let your room'.

My mother is not an advocate of the tactful approach. It transpired that she had answered an advertisement from the University and arranged to act as a landlady to two male students. This would give her an income of seventy pounds a week. Fifty pounds more than she receives from me. No contest. The two students (of engineering) are moving into my room on Friday afternoon. A new single bed has been purchased and is leaning accusingly against the wall of my bedroom.

Tuesday   June 14th

I found it hard to concentrate on my work today. The Head Librarian, Mrs Froggatt (fat, fifty and with the colouring and features of a jaundiced badger), said at lunchtime, 'Mole you've moved all our Jane Austens from the great English Classics section to the Light Romance Section, pray explain.' I snapped, 'In my opinion they have been given their proper classification. Jane Austen's novels are merely trashy romances read only by snobbish, brainless cretins.' How was I to know that 'Jane Austen, Her Genius, Her Relevance to England in the 1950's' was the subject of Mrs Froggatt's dissertation for her degree in English Literature many years before I was born? As I've said earlier in my diary, we didn't discuss books or writers in the library.

That afternoon I was called into Mrs Froggatt's room. She informed me that the library was cutting down on staff due to Governmental financial restraints. I asked how many staff would be asked to leave. 'Just the one,' said the Jane Austen admirer, 'and, since you were the last to come, Adrian, you must also be the first to go.' Homeless and jobless!

Wednesday   June 15th

When I got home from work, where I was shunned and vilified (it turned out that all the library staff like Jane Austen), I went to my room to find that my Mother had cleared out my toy cupboard. Pinky, my pink and grey rabbit, was nowhere to be seen! I burst into the kitchen, where my mother was entertaining her neighbours to tea. Through a thick smog of cigarette smoke I looked my mother in the eye and said, 'Where's Pinky?' 'He's outside in the dustbin,' she said. She had the grace to drop her eyes. She knew she'd done me and Pinky a terrible wrong. 'How could you?' I said coldly. I flung open the door that led to the yard. Pinky's threadbare ears were visible sticking out of a black plastic bag. I pulled him out of the bag and dusted him down, then I re-crossed the kitchen and slammed the door. Huge gusts of female laughter could be heard behind me as I ran up the stairs.

Pinky is exactly the same age as me. He was purchased by my drunken father on the day of my birth. Pinky only has, only ever had, two legs; but he is still a rabbit. It is beyond my comprehension how anyone could even *think* about disposing of him. I packed my suitcase there and then. I placed Pinky carefully in a carrier bag. I went into the kitchen. I addressed my mother. 'I'm going. I shall send for my books.' I went.

Thursday   June 16th

Living here with Sharon and eight other Botts is a nightmare. I am supposed to be sleeping on the living room couch but the Botts don't go to bed. They stop up, in the living room, talking and shouting and quarrelling and watching violent videos. A few Botts, Sharon was one, went to bed at 3am but the remaining Botts had noisy discussions about babies, contraception, menstruation, death, funerals, the price of ice-cream, Clement Freud, The Queen, the man in the moon, dogs, cats, gerbils, various aches and pains they had suffered from, clothes they had tired of. Then, after an hour of malicious gossip about a woman I'd never heard of called Cynthia Bell, I closed my eyes, feigning sleep. Would they take the hint and go to bed? No.

'Funny looking bugger isn't he?' said Mrs Bott. 'What does our Sharon see in him?'

Was she referring to me?

'He's supposed to be dead brainy,' said her eldest daughter Marjorie, 'though I ain't seen no evidence of brains. He just *sits* there looking like a wet weekend.'

'He's a randy little sod,' said Farah, the youngest Bott, 'our Sharon reckons 'e can do it four times a night.'

'Do what?' screeched Mrs Bott, 'thread a needle?'

The Botts screeched and cackled for quite some time then finally, after a lot of noisy stair climbing, went to bed. Dawn was breaking as I stretched out on the couch and went to sleep.

At 6am Mr Bott, a timid and, not surprisingly, quiet man, came into the living room and switched on breakfast television.

''Ope I'm not disturbin' you,' he said politely.

'Not at all,' I said. I got up, retrieved my suitcase from the hall, and walked out into the cool morning air.

I was on the first stage of my journey to Oxford, where I intended to fall on Pandora's neck and plead for sanctuary.

Friday   June 17th

It was lunchtime when I got to Pandora's flat. Pandora wasn't in. She was having a tutorial. However, a languorous youth called Julian Twyselton-Fife *was* in. We shook hands. I've grasped firmer rubber gloves.

To make conversation I asked him what he was doing at Oxford.

'Oh I'm just farting about,' he said airily. 'I shan't sit my finals, only people who intend to *work* do that.'

He offered me Turkish coffee. I accepted, not wanting to appear provincial. When it came I regretted my inferiority complex. I asked if he shared the flat with Pandora.

'I'm married to Pandora,' he said. 'She's Mrs Twyselton-Fife. I did it as a favour to her last week. Pandora has this dinky little theory that first marriages should be gotten over with quickly, so we intend to divorce quite soon. We don't *love* each other,' he added. Then, 'In fact, I prefer my own sex.' 'Good,' I said, 'because I intend to be Pandora's second husband.'

Pinky had slid out of his carrier bag. 'I say, who *is* that divine creature?' brayed Twyselton-Fife. He grasped Pinky to his tweedy bosom. I said, 'It's Pinky.'

He crooned, 'Oh Pinky, you're a handsome one, aren't you? Now, don't deny it, sir, accept the compliment!'

Pandora came in. She looked clever and lovely.

'Hello Mrs Twyselton-Fife.' I said.

'Oh, you know then?' she said.

'Can I stay here?' I asked.

'Yes,' she said.

So that was that. I am now in a *ménage à trois*. With a bit of luck it will soon be a *ménage à deux*. For ever.

Saturday   June 18th

I phoned home this morning. One of the engineering lodgers answered. 'Hello, Martin Muffet speaking.'

'Martin *Muffett*!' I said.

'Yes,' he said, 'and spare the jokes about tuffetts and spiders will you?'

'I wish to speak to my mother, Mrs Mole', I said.

'Pauline,' he bellowed before banging the phone down on the hall table. I heard the click of my mother's lighter, then she spoke.

'Adrian, where are you?'

'I'm in Oxford.'

'At the University?'

'Not *studying* at the University, no, that honour was denied me. If I'd had a complete set of Children's Encyclopedias perhaps I'd . . .'

'Oh don't start on that again. It's not my fault you didn't get your A' levels . . .'

'I'm here with Pandora and her husband.'

'*Husband?*'

I could image the expression on my mother's face. She would be looking like a starving dog which was being offered a piece of sirloin steak.

'Who? When? Why?' asked my mother, who in the unlikely event of being asked for her recreation by the publishers of *Who's Who*, would be honour bound to reply: 'My main recreation is gossiping.'

'Do Pandora's parents know that she's married?' asked my mother, still agog.

'No,' I replied. Then I thought, 'But it won't be long before they do, will it, mother?'

In the afternoon, Pandora and I went shopping. Julian Twyselton-Fife was lying in bed reading a Rupert Bear Annual. As we were leaving, he shouted, 'Don't forget the honey, darlings.'

Once we were outside, on the street, I told Pandora that she must start divorce proceedings. 'Right now, this minute.' I offered to accompany her to a solicitor's office.

'They don't work on Saturday afternoons,' she said. 'They play golf.'

'Monday morning,' I said.

'I've got a tutorial,' she said feebly.

'Monday afternoon,' I pressed.

'I'm having tea with friends,' she said.

'Tuesday morning?' I suggested.

We went through the whole week and then the following week. Pandora's every waking moment seemed to be accounted for. Eventually I exploded, 'Look Pandora, you do *want* to marry me don't you?'

Pandora poked at a courgette (we were in a greengrocer's shop at the time), then she sighed and said, 'Well actually darling, no; I don't intend to remarry until I'm at *least* thirty-six.

'*Thirty-six!*' I screeched. 'But, by then I could be fat or bald or toothless.'

Pandora looked at me and said, 'You're not exactly an Adonis *now*, are you?' In my hurry to leave the shop I knocked a pile of Outspan oranges onto the floor. In the resulting confusion (in which several old ladies reacted to the rolling oranges as though they were hand grenades, rather than mere fruit coming towards them), I failed to see Pandora leaving.

I ran after her. Then I felt a heavy hand on my shoulder, then a growling voice: the greengrocer's.

'Runnin' off without payin' eh?' Well I'm sick of you students nickin' my stuff, this time I'm prosecutin'. You'll be in a police cell tonight, my lad.'

It was with horror that I realised I had an Outspan orange in each hand.

Sunday   June 19th

I have been charged with shoplifting. My life is ruined. I shall have a criminal record. Now I will never get a job in the Civil Service.

Pandora is standing by me. She is feeling dead guilty because when *she* ran out of the shop she forgot to pay for a pound of courgettes, a lettuce and a box of mustard and cress.

Nothing has changed. It's still the rich what gets the gravy and the poor what gets the blame.

Mole at the Department of the Environment

July 1989

Monday   July 10th

I was called into Mr Brown's office today, but first I was kept waiting in the small vestibule outside. I noticed that Brown had allowed his rubber plant to die. I was scandalised by the sight of the poor, dead thing. Taking my penknife out of my pocket, I removed the decayed leaves until a brown, shrivelled stump was left.

Brown bellowed, 'Come'. So I went, though I was annoyed at being summond in like a dog.

Brown was looking out of the window and jiggling the change in his pocket. At least I *think* that was what he was doing, the only other possible alternative doesn't bear thinking about.

He turned and glowered at me. 'I have just heard a disquieting fact about you, Mole,' he said.

'Oh,' I said.

'Oh, indeed' repeated Brown. 'Is there something you should tell me about your lavatorial habits, Mole?'

After a period of thought I said. 'No sir, if it's about the puddle on the floor last Friday, that was when I . . .'

'No, no, not at work, at home,' he snapped. I thought about the lavatory at home. Surely I used it as other men did? Or did I? Was I doing something unspeakable without knowing it? And if I was how did Brown *know*?

'Think of your lavatory *seat* Mole. You have been heard bragging about it, in the canteen.' As I was bidden I thought about the newly installed lavatory seat at home.

'*Describe* the aforementioned lavatory seat, Mole.' I fingered my penknife nervously. Brown had obviously gone mad. It was common knowledge that he wandered around on motorway embankments at night, muttering endearments to hedgehogs.

'Well sir,' I said, edging imperceptibly towards the door. 'It's sort of a reddish brown wood, and it has brass fittings . . .' Brown shouted, 'Ha, reddish brown wood! . . . Mahogany! You are a vandal, Mole, an enemy of the earth. Consider your job to be on the line! Mahogany is one of the earth's most precious and endangered woods and you have further endangered it by your vanity and lust.'

Tuesday   July 11th

Pandora and I had an in-depth discussion about the mahogany lavatory seat tonight. It ended when she slammed the lid down angrily and said, 'Well, I like it; it's warm and comfortable, and it's staying!'

I have started scanning the job pages in *The Independent*.

Wednesday   July 12th

Brown has sent a memo round to all departments ordering the expulsion of all aerosols in the building. A spot check will be carried out tomorrow. The typing pool are in an ugly mood and are threatening mutiny.

Thursday   July 13th

There were pathetic scenes throughout the day as workers tried to hang on to their underarm deodorants and canisters of hairspray. But by four o'clock Brown announced a victory. It was a perspiring and limp-haired crowd of workers who left the building. Some shook their fists at the sky and swore at the ozone layer, or the lack of it. One or the other.

Friday   July 14th

BASTILLE DAY

Now there is trouble with the cleaning ladies! Apparently Brown has left a note in each of their mop-buckets ordering them to rid themselves of their Mr Sheen and Pledge. Mrs Sprogett who cleans our office was very bitter about Brown. ''E's askin' us to go back to the dark days of lavender wax,' she said. I tried to explain to the poor woman, but she said 'What's a bleedin' ozone layer when it's at home?'

Saturday   July 15th

Made a shocking discovery this morning. Our so called mahogany seat is made entirely of chip-board! I rang the bathroom fitments showroom and informed them that they had contravened the Trade Descriptions Act. I demanded a full refund.

Monday   July 16th

Went to Brown's office to appraise him of the latest facts regarding the lavatory seat, but he wasn't there. He has been suspended on full pay pending an enquiry into his wilful neglect and cruelty to a rubber plant.

Susan Lilian Townsend

Majorca

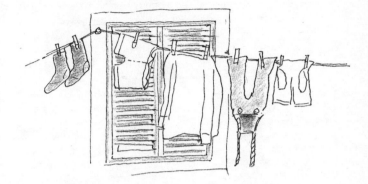

Week One

Thursday   29th October

The flight to Majorca is delayed. My boarding pass is rejected by a uniformed youth of thirteen.

> **Me:** 'Why?'
> **Youth:** 'Something's wrong with the plane.'
> **Me:** 'What *exactly* is wrong with the plane?'
> **Youth:** 'Dunno.'
> **Me:** 'How long before . . .?'
> **Youth:** 'Dunno.'

I predict a glittering future for the youth. Foreign Office spokesman is one job that comes to mind.

Although there are at least two hundred empty seats in the departure lounge, the majority of my fellow passengers begin to queue in front of the desk. Why? We have all been given our seat numbers for the aeroplane. There is a café only five yards away but few passengers break ranks and avail themselves of its facilities.

Some people stand for one hour and ten minutes *carrying*

heavy hand luggage. Not for them the luxury of placing it on the floor at their feet. Apart from it being communal airport neurosis, I cannot explain this perverse behaviour. Who says the English cannot be led into revolution? Get them inside an airport and they will follow any leader and have heads on pikestaffs quicker than you can say 'boarding card'.

Eventually we board the plane. The middle-aged couple next to me are wearing tweeds and are discussing their plans for Christmas – who to invite out: '*Certain* people will not be welcome, not after last year,' he says. My guess is that the 'certain people' are on her side of the family because she goes into a sulk. I don't exchange a word with this couple until we descend from the clouds above Majorca and I say aloud, 'Oh mountains!' He tells me that most of Majorca *is* mountains, which is why he and his wife love the island. 'The coast is hell for most of the year', he says.

We pass over red and green and black fields which together look like a vast Rastafarian draughtsboard, then hundreds of working windmills, and eventually Palma Bay, which looks like a child's drawing of the seaside: brilliant blue sea, custard coloured sand, white yachts and purple mountains in the background.

Within twenty minutes of landing I am in a taxi and speeding along the coast road. The taxi driver curses the other drivers. We pass an open truck which is full of roistering men waving bottles of wine about. They are middle-aged and conservatively dressed. They turn out to be English. The taxi driver smiles and says, '*Inglese*', as one might say 'madmen'.

'I have no knowledge of you', says the stern faced Manuel at hotel reception. 'You are not on the computer.' I showed him my reservation, pointed to the magic words 'confirmed' and 'telex'. He went into the back room. He picked up a phone. 'There is no room in the hotel', he said, returning from the savage sounding telephone conversation. I stood at the desk for twenty minutes. I sighed, I looked sad, I began to write in my notebook. Eventually he waved a large key at me and said, 'There is only one room'. I understood why when I got there. The plywood door stood ajar. The room was so unlovely that nobody in their right mind would want to steal anything at all from it. The décor was in shades of suicide brown, the lighting was to Albanian specifications. There was an appalling smell, as though a disease-wracked creature had died and been decomposing behind the skirting board for some months. I sprinkled duty free perfume about like a high Anglican priest; the smell got worse. On such occasions I count my blessings: 1: I'm alive. 2: I'm almost healthy. 3: I'm not in a car on the Birmingham Inner Ring Road.

I changed out of my English woollens and into my daughter's Bermuda shorts. I looked in the mirror. First the front view; not bad, Townsend. Then the back view; grotesque, Townsend. Take them off, woman.

Twelve floors down, Spanish women were strolling in the street, elegantly attired in tailored suits and high heels.

I inspected my holiday clothes. Had somebody, some mad person with a grudge against me, broken into my house the night before and thrown my carefully co-ordinated clothes away, and replaced them with this bizarre collection? How else to explain the presence in my luggage of an ankle length, beige linen circular skirt, *jewelled* espadrilles, *two* evening bags. Bloodstained blue and orange sandals. A size sixteen sundress (I am size twelve). Harem trousers over-printed with (possibly insulting) Spanish phrases. How did my daughter's old school cardigan get in there?

It was in the jewelled espadrilles and a cotton pyjama suit with an evening bag slung across my chest that I left the hotel and went for a walk. As I left the hotel my sunglasses fell off and broke on the pavement. I walked twenty-five yards and sat down at a pavement café. After a quick repair job on the sunglasses I ordered coffee and read my guide book: *Majorca*, English edition by Antonio Cammpana and Juan Puig-Ferran.

> '*Dear Friends and Readers, if you are or imagine you are a victim of neurasthenia, deafened and confused by the noise of our modern civilisation and the urge to arrive more quickly at some place where you have nothing to do, and if business has filled with numbers the space in your brain that is intended for what we call intelligence; if the cinema has damaged your optic organism, and the flickering has become chronic, and restlessness and worry will not let you live, and you want to enjoy a little of the rest to which anybody in this world is entitled who has done no harm to anyone – then follow me to an island where calm always reigns and men are never in a hurry, where the women*

*never grow old, where words are not wasted, where the sun
stays longer than anyhere else and the Lady Moon moves
more slowly, sleepy with idleness.*
  This island, dear Readers, is Majorca.'
  Santiago Rusinol.

Using my 'optic organisms' I see many taxis passing by with
signs behind the windscreens saying 'libre'. I flag one down and
ask for Palma Nova. I have a reason for wanting to visit Palma
Nova; my daughter and her friend spent two weeks there in July.
They have dined out on it since. A hotel barman had stripped all
his clothes off, then ran into the lift and shouted, just before the
doors closed, 'Who wants me?' Nobody – as it turned out. Then
there was the incident of the quarrelling honeymoon couple who
had a fist fight in the hotel dining room (he ordered her to sell
her horse on their return to England, she refused saying that she
loved the horse far more than she loved him).

Worst of all were the battalions of drunken young European
men who kept up a twenty four hour chant of ''ere we go, 'ere
we go.' As some fell asleep, chanting, others rose from their beds
and carried on. Remember this was in July.

On the October afternoon I was there the loudest noises came
from the construction gangs singing as they worked on the new
buildings. The beaches were deserted, as were the cafés and bars.
The shops were devoid of any customers. A few elderly people
strolled along the promenades. I went for a paddle; the sea was
clear and warm. Unable to resist it I went for a swim. I hadn't
brought a towel but it didn't matter. I lay on the sand and was
dry in ten minutes. Both sides.

When the sun went down, promptly and spectacularly at 6pm,
I caught a bus back to Palma. This took me into the city centre
where I got lost. In my opinion it is essential to get lost in a new
city, that way you are forced to walk about and discover places at
a proper, natural pace. But you must have the taxi fare home,
and it helps if you can remember the name of your hotel.

I wandered into the old part of the city and began a happy
exploration of the winding alleys and steep narrow streets full of
shops. The smell of leather filled the air. Palma has almost as
many shoe shops as Leicester, so I felt quite at home. Eventually
the jewelled espadrilles began to pinch so I flagged a taxi down

on *Jaime III*, which is Palma's equivalent to Regent Street, and went back to the hotel.

I dined in a Chinese restaurant which had no chopsticks on the premises. Everything came covered in Lee and Perrins sauce. A Chinese man stood at the door shaking hands with incoming customers. He had the sense not to attempt the same with outgoing customers. When the kitchen door opened I could see the Spanish cooks toiling over their woks.

Thus ended the first day.

Friday   30th October

I walked thirteen miles today. It took me eight hours. I set out to look at the Cathedral, a magnificent building which dominates the bay. As it happened the nearest I got to the cathedral was sitting on the terrace of a café opposite. I felt disinclined to miss any of the hot sunshine so I walked along the promenade admiring the flowering shrubs and trees. I stopped for a swim on an empty beach closely watched by three ancient gardeners who were sprinkling and watering grass seed onto the verge of the road.

They shouted encouragement as I swam (I think it was encouragement) and waved goodbye when I collected my things and headed away from them. At this point a little white dog joined me. I am frightened of most English dogs owing to their unpredictable tempers, but Majorcan strays displayed nothing but good-natured curiosity – they fought amongst themselves occasionally but I never saw them bother humans apart from butchers, whose doorways they haunted.

I talked to the mangy dog as we walked along the very edge of the bay. I told him that I was also alone and hadn't spoken more than a few words to anyone for over thirty-six hours. He looked sympathetic. Together we crossed irrigation channels, and bridges. We detoured up side roads passing shut up holiday villas. For some alarming miles we walked along a busy dual carriageway until we found a route back to the sea. We stopped at a restaurant and I ordered an excellent paella. I was the only customer. The dog sat under the table begging for scraps for a while, and then went to sleep. The proprietor *forced* me into having a drink with him – he wanted to tell me that he'd visited London several times and thought it was 'very good place'. He asked me if my husband was 'dead'. I told him 'no'. He asked if my husband was 'gone'. I told him no. Eventually I extricated myself from him with some difficulty and, leaving the dog asleep, I walked on without stopping until I came to C'an Pastilla which is a seaside resort blessed with wide sandy beaches, numerous shops and cafés, and conveniently placed pedestrian crossings. I mention the crossings because a dual carriageway runs along this part of the coast. Two elderly English women strolled along the beach, arm in arm, confessing lifelong resentments: 'John was tetchy for forty years.'

'So was Ron, for forty-one.'

It gladdened my heart to see so many elderly people in the autumn sunlight. You could almost *see* arthritic bones mending, backs straightening and complexions tanning. There were many pensioners swimming in the sea and sunbathing on the beach, and, later that evening, getting very drunk in the bars.

I journeyed on and at some point C'an Pastilla merged and then became Arenal, and as night fell the sound of the dreaded electric organ began to drift up from basement bars. Arenal belonged to the German elderly. They strolled along the pavements, hand in pudgy hand, trying to decide where to eat. I ate on the terrace of an Italian restaurant; 1,000 pesetas for soup, bread, salad, tagliatelli, two glasses of Torres, dry white wine, one bottle of mineral water, three cups of cafe con leche. The night was warm and the food was good, and I decided that I liked Majorca. I caught a bus back into Palma (75 pesetas) and was in bed by nine-thirty.

Saturday   31st October

Today I went in the opposite direction, to Illetas. I caught a bus behind my hotel in Palma and twenty minutes later I got off the bus and found myself in Paradise. Illetas is where the rich spend their holidays. The villas and hotels are magnificent and the foliage is even more abundant.

I walked up and down a hilly road until I came to a sign which said, 'to the beach'. I then walked through a gate and into the Garden of Eden. I passed a woman cleaning the shutters of a holiday villa with a wet sweeping brush, then I walked down a twisting path shaded by palms and hibiscus through which could be seen the unnaturally blue sea. Ahead of me I saw a youth –

whom I took to be a young gardener pruning a bush; the leaves were shaking and scarlet petals were falling. The youth saw me approach and stepped from behind the bush. It was *not* a pair of secateurs in his hands, he was holding something quite different. I stood very still. He sat down on the raised edge of the pathway. There was nobody else about.

'Put it away', I said in brisk English tones. He took his hands away and shrugged his shoulders, as if to say 'You can see the state I'm in, what can I do?' I shouted 'Senora!' to the woman cleaning the shutters. She didn't turn round, perhaps she was a senorita. The youth continued his urgent manipulations. I didn't know where to look but I was too scared to turn my back on him, and I was damned if he was going to stop me getting to the beach.

'Bad boy', I said.

Suddenly three little children ran down the path. Before I could stop them they saw the youth. They turned back. A little girl began to cry. I was furious then. I shouted to the youth, who ran away holding his jeans in one hand, and himself in the other. He ran past the children, who screamed.

An old gardener came trudging up the path. He saw the fear on my face. I tried to explain. The gardener gave a spirited mime of what he thought had happened (rather too spirited in fact), then he saw the youth and ran towards him shouting violently. I carried on down the glorious pathway and found a perfect cove at the bottom.

A guitarist in the beach bar was serenading a German family with the 'birdie song', the father joined in, he was tone deaf. His wife and children looked embarrassed and tried to cover the discordant noise he was making by singing very loudly. But the guitarist did a cruel imitation of the father. Everyone laughed, including me, I'm ashamed to say. I swam and sunbathed and noticed lone men dotted amongst the greenery on the slopes of the cove. They were fully dressed and staring down at the young topless lying on the beach. One man scrambled down and began to take photographs of the girls. A German father objected violently and the man ran back up the slope. I stayed on the beach until the sun went down, then I ran back up the pathway and got the bus back to Palma where Spanish children were running amok with garlands of sweets around their necks. A

Saints Day celebration. I got happily lost for two hours then went back to the hotel and after passing the Fattest Man in Spain, who was checking into the hotel, I went to my room and to sleep.

Sunday   1st November

The Fattest Man in Spain has a thin, beautiful wife; she goes to and fro between the hotel breakfast buffet and her husband's mouth. She brings platefuls and bowlfuls and cupfuls and glassfuls until, eventually, he is satisfied. She then helps him to his feet and they leave the room.

He, she and me, together with thirty-four other people are booked on a coach tour. We are going to see the Pearl Factory in Manacor, the Caves of Drach near to Porto Cristo, and an Olive Wood Factory. Our guide is young and handsome and cynical. He tells us in bitter tones that there were eleven million 'traffic' passing through Palma airport this year. He means tourists. He is also distressed by the convoluted olive trees we pass. 'Look at them', he cries. 'Awful! The peasants don't know how to look after them! Old, dirty!' On the road we pass a bar, now called 'Reagan' but previously called 'Carter' and before that 'Kennedy'. Will it one day be called 'Quayle'?

After only twenty minutes of travelling, the coach stops outside a mega souvenir shop and sherry warehouse. I like a shop as much as the next woman but there is nothing, nothing I wish to buy here. We next stop at the Pearl Factory in Manacor, but it is Sunday and apart from two sad-looking employees, nobody is working. We file past empty work benches where the girls' aprons are slung just as they left them, no doubt in their eagerness to get away from the pearls. We are encouraged to go into the huge retail shop but I don't buy anything, pearls are too redolent of the Queen and Mrs Thatcher. I sit outside in the sun instead.

We drive on to Porto Cristo and are told we should eat in a certain restaurant (lunch is not included in the price of the excursion). I decide not to eat there and instead go round the corner and have what the waiter recommends, which turns out to be a huge fish with more bones than flesh. Remembering the Queen Mother's misfortune I abandon the fish and go to look for the sea. I spend the next half an hour sitting on a headland surrounded by sweet-smelling thyme. The sea is far below. It is perfectly quiet and very lovely. I sit and dangle my legs over the edge of the cliff and there is nobody there to tell me to 'Come away from the side!' Then I go to see the caves of Drach. The floors and steps are wet and very slippery, an old man in front of me falls and bangs his head, his son kneels over him with touching concern. Of the cave I will say very little. A cave is a cave is a cave.

I didn't buy anything at the Olive Wood factory either. Can this be the same woman who was ordered at gunpoint out of the Duty Free Shop at Moscow airport? Yes, it is. I've learned my lesson. Travel light. Olive wood is very heavy. I ate dinner in the hotel dining room.

'Solo?' asked the Maître D.

'Yes.' I reply. It seems like an admission of failure. I sit behind a pillar and watch the Fattest Man in Spain eat his dinner. He has a lovely face and a Rolex watch.

Monday   2nd November

I wait for a bus to Calvia. A man draws his car alongside me. He says, 'I am Antonio, what is your name?' Foolishly I answer, 'Susan'.

> **Antonio:** 'Good now we are friends. Now Susan get into my car.'
> **Susan:** 'No, Antonio, I won't.'
> **Antonio:** 'Yes you will Susan, get into the car.'
> **Susan:** 'I'm going on the bus.'
> **Antonio:** 'Where, Susan?'
> **Susan:** 'I will not tell you, Antonio.'
> **Antonio:** 'You are stupid, Susan.'
> **Susan:** 'So are you, Antonio.'
> **Antonio:** 'Goodbye, Susan.'
> **Susan:** 'Goodbye, Antonio.'

Calvia is a lovely green-shuttered town surrounded by mountains. It was four o'clock when I arrived. Nobody was on the steep streets. The shops were closed. According to my guide book the inhabitants of Calvia habitually indulged in loud communal conversations. It took twenty minutes to walk around the little town, including a visit to the Cathedral, which is distinguished by having a clock on each side of its tower (none of which shows the correct time). At five I was ready to leave. I stood at the bus stop in the main square. At six I was still there. It got cold. An old Englishman with a walrus moustache approached me and inexplicably asked me if I needed water. 'I've got ten ten-gallon drums in here', he said, proving it by lifting the boot of his car. I thanked him but declined the water. He then offered me a lift 'half-way' to Palma; again I declined. I was still sitting by the bus-stop at half past six. By now the streets were full of chattering Calvians. A slow-witted young man was lurching up and down the main street uttering inarticulate cries. He came up to me, pulled me to my feet, and gestured towards the bottom of the hill. I sat down, he pulled me up. I sat down again. Eventually he gave up and lurched off. At seven-thirty I was told by an ironmonger that the bus was not coming to the square. On its return journey it left from the bottom of the hill just as the slow-witted man had tried to tell me. I braved entering an all-male bar and asked the barman for help. He kindly rang for a taxi and then gave me a Cointreau and ice on the house. Calvians are exceptionally nice people.

Safely back in Palma I ate in a Chinese restaurant. Jimmy Young was singing 'They tried to tell us we're too young', in the background.

I've changed my hotel room. I now have a balcony which overlooks Palma Bay. The view is magical.

Tuesday   3rd November

At breakfast I sit surrounded by at least twenty empty tables. However, an English couple choose a table so close to me that I have to move my chair in order to accommodate them. They both have braying upper middle-class accents.

> **She:** 'Is that all you're eating, fruit?'
> **He:** 'Yes.'
> **She:** 'Did you see the boiled eggs?'
> **He:** 'Boiled eggs?'
> **She:** 'Yes, they're in a little basket next to those roll things.'
> **He** (*obviously lying*): 'I saw them but I don't want one.'
> **She** (*astonished*): 'But you always have a boiled egg, Clive.'
> **He:** 'I don't want one today.'

She: 'Aren't you well?'

He (*angry*): 'I'm perfectly well.'

She: 'Shall I get some coffee?'

He: 'Not if it's real.'

She: 'It is.'

He: 'Then I shan't have any.'

She: 'For the whole fortnight?'

He: 'Yes, for the whole bloody fortnight.'

She: 'Oh Clive, don't be like this, not on the first day.'

He: 'Just because I don't want a bloody boiled egg!'

He was wearing black socks and sandals. If I were an airport official I would have confiscated Clive's socks at customs control.

I lunched in Palma in the Plaza Major. A violent wind blows up suddenly and sends the parasols and tablecloths and tourist menus (475 pesetas) flying across the marble floor. While I am eating my paella an old man asks me if I want my shoes shined, he shows me a tin of black polish. I demur; I am wearing blue suede shoes.

In the old part of the city I see a beautiful leather bag. I buy it. It is so wonderful that I plan to throw it open to the public: admission £1. Sundays only. No dogs. No children. No photographs.

I have a drink in the hotel bar before dinner. An Englishman, who looks like a cartoon crook, asks me if I like the song, 'As Time Goes By'.

'Of course,' I say. 'Who doesn't?'

'I'll get the band to play it for yer, when you've 'ad yer' dinner,' he says.

As I leave the dining room I hear: 'You must remember this . . .' being crooned into a microphone. I scuttle to the lift before crook-face can get off his bar stool.

Week 2

Wednesday   4th November
PORTO SOLLER

Manuel, the hotel receptionist, tells me that the train to Porto Soller, on the west side of the island, leaves at 1pm. However the taxi driver who is taking me to the railway station lies and says, 'No more trains today, winter service. I take you, very cheap, 2,700 pesetas.'

I am known for my gullibility, so I agreed and we embark on a most exciting mountain drive, during which the driver points out interesting sights such as an occasional car at the bottom of the chasm. However he drives very carefully on the mad, convoluted roads and acts as my guide and Spanish teacher; he also asks me if my husband is dead. 'I hope not', I say and laugh, rather too loudly and for too long. I am missing laughing and talking.

'You have children?' he asks.

'Yes four,' I reply.

'Not possible,' he says, politely.

Only *too* possible, dearie, I think.

After half an hour we start to descend and the driver tells me that the large town in the valley before us is Soller and was built inland in an attempt to avoid the nuisance of attacks by pirates. We then drive one and a half kilometers to the coast to Porto Soller, and I immediately like this small holiday resort with its palm trees and its clean beach and its out of season booted German hikers carrying long walking poles. A lovely tram rattles between the Port and the town through orchards of orange and lemon trees and lush back gardens. The tram stops outside the prettiest railway station in the world. Amongst other delights it has a vine-covered bar, an accurate station clock and spanking green and gilt paintwork on the platform.

I seriously covet a pair of gilted angel's heads I see in a shop window near to the station, but I am never to find the shop open again. The inhabitants of Soller are stomping about in wellingtons because a light drizzle is falling. I buy a kilo of mandarins complete with green leaves, 175 pesetas. I have coffee, 100 pesetas, and catch the tram back to Porto Soller. I overhear two English business women talking. One says, 'The trouble with David is, he uses too many commas.'

'For a finance manager', says her companion.

Thursday   5th November

The sun has gone to my head. I've just gone into a bank and asked for 10,000 pizzas.

'You must go to a restaurant,' says the cashier, laughing, before giving me my 10,000 pesetas. I swim and sunbathe on the beach and then return to the hotel and wait for the photographer who is flying out from England today. I hope he won't constantly whine about 'the light', like most photographers do.

Friday   6th November

The photographer, Barry, is extremely nice, he doesn't whine once, he isn't a bore, and he is enthusiastic about Porto Soller. He charms people into helping him. A lugubrious Frenchman is seduced away from his sunbed and asked to hold a portable light, and the deckchair man, Pedro, poses happily. He tells us not to come in the season, 'children cry, sun hot hot hot. Many people, disco noise all night.' According to the deckchair man the best months are May and September.

Saturday   7th November

Barry and I drive to Valldemosa, the monastery retreat of Georges Sand and Chopin. Ms. Sand was hoping for a *grand amour*, but Chopin immediately fell ill, the weather was appalling and the local people took against her and her entourage. They were unused to seeing a trousered cigar-smoking female in the vicinity. Her description of Valldemosa and the surrounding countryside as written in *A Winter in Majorca* is so perfect that I cannot equal it, but only urge you to read the book and visit Valldemosa for yourself. The high-walled gardens behind each monk's cell are a special delight.

Sunday   8th November

The rain is pouring down; disconsolate Germans sit about in the hotel, twiddling their sticks. Barry leaves for England and I decide to hire a taxi for the afternoon and go to Calobra to see the Torrent de Pareis, a natural phenomenon, where the sea enters between massive cliffs and forms a river. Apart from a thin strip of sand the beach consists of small, sharp pebbles. The Torrent is amazing but the drive to it is quite incredible. We pass desolate wildernesses, mountain top reservoirs, and fields of petrified trees which look like creatures from Fantasia. The taxi dodges falling rocks, sudden springs of water, sheep, deer and goats, shaking foreign drivers in hire cars, and, once, a car pulling a *caravan*. 'Give that man a medal', I thought, as I watched the driver navigate around a crumbling hair pin bend, while my heart did a fandango and Mrs Caravan shut her eyes. These are serious roads. As a woman said in the car park at the bottom of the mountain 'I couldn't have stood another minute.'

In the late afternoon I walked to the top of the cliffs in Porto Soller, and as the light faded I climbed a rock face in my jewelled espadrilles. It was an extremely stupid thing to do.

Monday   9th November

Today I left Porto Soller. I got on the tram and then caught a train to Palma from the loveliest railway station in the world, and I don't mind admitting it, Watson, I had tears in my eyes. I will be back as soon as time and the Inland Revenue allow.

Majorca is magnificent – out of season.

Writing for Television

Last year I had the efficiency of my nerve ends tested in a hospital Out Patients Department. I was hooked up to a machine and then had a series of electric shocks administered to my fingers and arms. The female doctor had a Viennese accent, the technician in charge of the machinery was silent throughout. When I closed my eyes (which I did frequently) I fancifully thought myself in Nazi Germany, bravely withstanding torture. After the two-hour ordeal had finished, I swore *never* again.

I feel much the same way about writing for television. Why put myself through it? It always starts out pleasantly – usually lunch or dinner in a good restaurant. The wine is slopped into your glass in great quantities by the producer. He doesn't mention the project you're about to embark on until the coffee arrives. All previous conversation has been about the house he is renovating. He has told you about his appalling childhood, his allergies, his delinquent children. He has taken you blow by blow through his first marriage. Occasionally he listens while you speak the odd sentence.

Then, the coffee poured out, comes the purpose of your meeting: the script. He takes it out of his briefcase, he weighs it in his hand. He pulls a face, 'Of course it's too long', he says. 'The scenes on the beach will have to go'.

'But', you say, 'It's called, *The Beach*. The whole point of the piece is that it's set on a beach.'

'Beaches are always difficult,' he says. 'Sand in the camera lens.' 'How about *The Field*?' He then talks for twenty-five minutes on the advantages of resetting your piece in a field. You find yourself (in spite of attending twelve one-hour assertiveness training sessions) agreeing to this daft notion.

'Now,' he says, 'characters. I don't believe in Tom.'

'Why?' you ask. 'Tom is an English working-class man in love with a middle-class woman, they meet on the beach, sorry, field.' The producer says, 'I think Tom should be an American, a tourist.'

You reel about in your chair and knock back the brandy you'd previously refused. He speaks for ten minutes about this new, American, Tom. 'Obviously,' he says, 'Tom can't be a council dustman now, can he? Perhaps you could give him a more glamorous job – journalist, actor, stockbroker?'

You flick mournfully through your script, reminding yourself that half of the action takes place at the Council Cleansing Depot in Clacton-Next-The-Sea. How can you possibly transfer these scenes to other, more glamorous, locations?

The producer has the answer, 'Change the location to County Cork in Ireland,' he suggests.

At this latest shock your first instinct is to cry out for more brandy, your second instinct is to flee from the restaurant taking your script with you, but you stay where you are. You hear yourself agreeing to rewrite the script. *The Field*, starring American Tom and set in County Cork in Ireland. What's more you have promised to deliver the rewrites in five days, because the producer is going on holiday (he has a cottage in County Cork, coincidentally) and would like to work on the rewrites 'away from the office'.

He then suggests that Amanda, whom you describe in your script as 'tall and slim and patrician', is two dimensional. 'Wouldn't it be better if she was a short, earthy blonde?'

At this point you are joined at the table by the producer's wife, a short, earthy blonde. She tells you that she adores your script. She is dyslexic, but her husband read it aloud to her last night. The blonde tells you she is an actress, she hasn't worked for years because there is a conspiracy in the industry to keep her out of work. She blames this on the 'pinko-communists, who are running the business'. Asked to name a communist she says, 'Michael Grade.' After you have stopped laughing, you realise that the producer's wife wants to play the part of your heroine. She has turned up at the restaurant for this reason. She has brought along her scrapbook. You peer with a fixed smile at photographs of the producer's wife playing Juliet at Kettering Rep 1957, Second Policewoman on the set of Dixon of Dock Green 1962, and back end of cow, Dick Whittington, Haringey Civic Hall 1985.

When the producer lumbers off to the lavatory, the producer's wife clutches your hand, she confides that her life with 'him' is a torment; if only she could earn enough money to leave him. Your feminist sympathies are stirred. You agree that she is perfect for the part. You give it to her, then instantly regret it. You leave the restaurant (after paying the bill) and look for a taxi. You do not want to ride in the taxi, only to throw yourself under the wheels, but luck is not with you, no taxi comes, so you go home, sit at your desk and like the good girl that you are, you do the rewrites.

Russia

When I told my second son that I was going to Russia he narrowed his eyes and said, 'Again?' He went off on some mysterious late-adolescent errand and on his return said, 'After you're dead, I won't be surprised to be told that you weren't really a writer (the cruelty of youth), you were a spy'. This made me laugh quite a lot. Spying, as a profession, seems to me about as interesting and useful as designing horse blankets for 'My Little Pony'. In my ideal world there would be an annual spies' convention held in a large hotel. Secrets would be swapped openly in the lobbies and bars; so much more comfortable than hanging around on street corners; cheaper too, in the long run.

He was suspicious because it was to be my third visit to Russia. The first time I went to find Dostoyevsky's grave. I'd fallen for him at the impressionable age of fourteen. If he'd been alive in 1961 I would have stood outside his lodging house badgering him for an autograph and begging for a clipping from his beard.

My second visit was with my husband, in winter. The tour was called, 'The Cities of the Golden Ring'. Five English people travelled the snowy landscape in a large coach full of diesel fumes. Frequently the fuel froze in the tank and the driver thawed it out with a flaming rolled-up *Pravda*. Nobody believes me but we occasionally ate like kings and queens. We also saw ninety billion icons – my husband suffered from iconophobia; visiting Woolworth's art department on our return was the only cure.

My last visit was in May of this year. I was a guest of the Great Britain-USSR Association. There was only one serious drawback, I would be in the company of other writers. The purpose of the visit was to have round table talks with members of the Soviet Writers' Union.

I am scared of writers, and, fearful of their beady-eyed scrutiny, I normally avoid literary occasions. But because it was Russia I accepted.

The visa was applied for. I read the list of the accompanying writers with a sinking heart. Paul Bailey, Alan Bennett, Timothy Mo, Craig Raine and Christopher Hope. I had nothing against them as *people* – I'd never met them – but they *were* writers. We met for lunch at the Great Britain-USSR headquarters in Grosvenor Place. John Roberts, the association's director, introduced us to Anne Vaughan, who was to be our mother, timekeeper, guide, translator, travel organiser, and lender of tights. During lunch I overheard Timothy Mo say, 'I hope to get some scuba diving in'. 'In Moscow?' I thought. It reminded me of a friend of mine who was summoned to the Job Centre, where he informed the clerk that he hadn't worked for several years because he was a sponge diver but he didn't want to leave Leicester.

As we got on to the plane Timothy Mo remarked in a loud voice 'Oh this is the plane that bits keep falling off of'. Ungrammatical, but devastating in its effect on Alan Bennett, who is not fond of hurtling through the air in a potential metal coffin. There was a long delay; eventually Dave Platt, the pilot, spoke to us. Mr Bennett pricked up his ears. In decidedly over-cheerful tones Dave told us of the problems in getting the plane from the hangar; we were now stacking and would soon be off. Mr Bennett's knuckles took on an unhealthy hue. I had left my books in my luggage. I had nothing to read but *Highlife*. I read all the articles then turned in desperation to the advertisements. One in particular caught my attention. '*Security, Surveillance, Survival:* the briefcase that sees everything!' And another, '*Privacy Protection:* don't let business associates or spouses intrude on your privacy. The VL34 privacy protector finds bugs and transmitters that may be hidden *right now* in your hotel room, office, home or car'.

I looked around at my fellow passengers and wondered how many, if any, were sufficiently paranoid as to be lugging their privacy protectors to Moscow.

The ceiling at Sherimetievo airport is decorated with thousands of what look like bottomless baking tins, only a few of which contained light bulbs. We met up with our translators, Galina and Nina and, eventually, Christopher Hope who had joined us from another writers' conference in Vienna. We groped our way out of the murk and breathed in the Russian air; a mixture of diesel fumes, sewage and something sweet. I love the country so I may have imagined the something sweet. On the way to Moscow, Galina pointed out where the German tanks had been stopped, only twenty kilometres from the city, during what the Russians call the Great Patriotic War. The next day I overheard an English woman say, 'They should have got over the war by now'. As though the loss of twenty million people was a trivial matter, to be compared to a nasty attack of chickenpox. A whole generation still exist who venerate the memory of their family and their friends who fought against fascism and never returned home. The Great Patriotic War remains a living memory. The past is still the present. There are fresh flowers on every war memorial in Russia every day of the year.

Our hotel was one of seven monolithic buildings that Stalin ordered to be constructed to represent the seven points of the communist star. Our particular point of the star was called 'The Ukraine'. Massive and stolid, it towers over the river Moskva looking like a cartoon from Gotham city. There was the traditional booking muddle, and for the first night people were forced to share rooms. Alan Bennett and Paul Bailey occupied a suite of rooms complete with piano and dining table. It was round this table that we sat, and had a supper of twiglets, liquorice allsorts, lemon vodka and champagne. We needed refreshment because we'd been to Red Square and then spent half an hour crouching with laughter at the window displays in Gum, the largest department store in Moscow. As Alan Bennett said, 'Well what can you *do* with two dozen packets of baby's rusks. It would test the ingenuity of even the most fashionable window dresser'. This was the first of many laughing, crouching sessions. We seemed to spend most of the time bent double, a little gang of hunchbacks, with streaming eyes and stamping feet. As many

Russians were to say to us, 'We thought the English were cold, reserved people but you are all so jolly'. Jolly no, hysterical yes. Most of us regressed steadily throughout the trip. I was six years old on my return to England, I needed help with my shoe-laces.

After the last liquorice was eaten a rat ran underneath the piano so we left Mr Bailey and Mr Bennett and went to bed. Our first meeting at the Soviet Writers' Union headquarters gradually took a surreal turn. After introductions and short speeches we launched into our discussion topic. 'Does the past influence how we write?' On the table stood bottles of coca-cola and saucers full of fondant sweets. Craig Raine opened the batting for England, his discourse, spoken in his lovely querulous voice, was very well received. After everyone present had spoken, the Russian chairperson, head of the School of Journalism at Moscow University, suggested, in his perfect English, that we break for coffee. We all perked up and trooped outside to the lobby. However, though promised, no coffee appeared, in fact nothing appeared so we trooped back inside for the final session of that day. We were well into our stride, the words 'perestroika' and 'glasnost' were tripping off our tongues. When Sakharov, the great Soviet playwright appeared, he seemed to be in a bad mood. He opened his newspaper and started to read. This was slightly disconcerting and had the effect of drawing every eye to him. I was particularly fascinated by the colour of his skin. I had seen that tint before, surely it was Max Factor panstick; natural beige?

Sakharov spoke briefly about his play, *Onward, Onward, Onward*. Then got up and left. The next day's session was much more interesting. For a start there were great slabs of spam and cheese sandwiches on the table. Sakharov came in and opened his newspaper but this time he read aloud, from an article attacking bureaucracy. Sakharov spoke passionately about the old men who had dominated the Soviet Writers' Union for many years. He said they were dead wood preventing the growth of new trees. He said they wouldn't retire and refused to die. Katya, a translator and expert on Joyce spoke excitedly about the possibilities now open to writers, it was as though she couldn't wait to start. Her pen twitched in her hand.

My favourite person was a poet; he was small and pale and had a lisp. He was once a professor of mathematics but after ten years he grew bored with doing his sums and instead turned to writing humorous verse. Another writer had worked in nuclear physics but failed to find the romance he had expected and had taken up the more difficult career of play-writing. I asked how many humorous books had been published during Stalin's tenure in the Kremlin. 'One' was the reply.

It was impossible not to respect and admire our Soviet counterparts. They had persevered and waited for their time to come, and now it was almost here, and we were there to witness the crack in the door.

For the record: according to Timothy Mo, Sakharov's skin colour was his own. More bran needed in his diet, suggests Nurse Townsend.

One night we dined in a private co-operative restaurant used by The Soviet Writers Union. A noisy party entered and sat at an adjacent table. The men were oldish, the women were beautiful. Yevtushenko, the Billy Fury of Russian poetry, was amongst the party. (He was big in the sixties, toured Britain wearing a leather cap, remember him?) Yevtushenko is now ravaged-looking, his hair, which used to flop insolently over one eye like Tallulah Bankhead's now sticks up around his head like that of a recently woken baby. He had taken drink before his arrival and proceeded to take more – quite a lot more. His voice got louder, his companions became glazed-eyed. He turned his chair around. 'English woman, give me a cigarette.' 'If you give me wine,' I said. I took him a fag and an empty glass. I returned with the empty glass. Later, much, much later, Christopher Hope and I were waiting outside on the pavement for a taxi when a woman writer and her companions got out of a flash car. Earlier in the day this woman had swept into the round table discussions dressed in Italian designer clothes, she had spoken at great mind-numbing length about her life and work. Paul Bailey had passed a note; 'She thinks a lot of herself', it said. She recognised the elegantly dressed Christopher Hope. 'Robert Redford is coming', she enthused. Apparently the great heart-throb was in Moscow and had promised to join her and Yevtushenko's party, which now included the great director of *Crime and Punishment*, only recently returned to Russia after being in exile. No taxi appeared; Christopher and I returned to the restaurant and were given a consoling bottle of wine – previously refused. Robert Redford's chair and that of his companions stood empty and waiting, and remained empty and waiting. He stood them up.

Yevtushenko grew even more boisterous, his companions more silent. He started to prowl around the restaurant bellowing verse. He stopped at our table. 'Give me more cigarette', he demanded. He was given a second fag. 'I smoke it, I chew it, I destroy it'. He proclaimed. The next day an article about the dangers of alcoholism appeared in Pravda – written by Yevtushenko. Christopher and I laughed long and hard on hearing this.

Throughout our stay we were privileged visitors and travelled everywhere in private hire cars. Craig Raine said, 'God I feel guilty sitting in this limo don't you?' Alan Bennett said, 'Yes, but it's swiftly erased.'

The cars enabled us to get around easily. We visited the private market where Anne and I were each presented with a single red carnation by a handsome Georgian market trader. We spent a morning in an art gallery where two Matisses, 'The Painter's Studio', and 'Still Life with Goldfish', hung on the walls radiating brilliance and simplicity. More sombre but resounding with humanity was Van Gogh's 'Prisoners at Exercise'. Outside the gallery a huge queue had formed of people wishing to buy tickets for the forthcoming Salvador Dali exhibition. Passing by was a clichéd homosexual with permed hair, hand on hip and a defiant expression on his hunter's face.

The cars delivered us to the cemetery where the great and good Chekhov is buried. Galina asked the man guarding the gate if we could enter. 'No', he said.

'But I have six British writers here,' she protested.

'So what?' he replied. 'I am a *reader*. They can't come in.'

We admired the man's comic timing but after we had stopped laughing we were infuriated by his jobsworth attitude – reminiscent of British Rail staff at Brighton Station. We could only gaze through the bars and reflect that Chekhov would have enjoyed the joke. We passed Melvyn Bragg, who was working as a doorman at the Ukraine Hotel, and left to catch an overnight train to Orel in Central Russia. Orel was the home of many important writers – albeit briefly – most of them hot-footed it to Moscow as soon as they were published. We were met by representatives of the Soviet Writers' Union, and driven to the Shipkta Motel which was set amongst birch woods. After breakfast we toured the town. Our guide wore pop socks and Minnie Mouse court shoes and eagerly pointed out the confluence of the two rivers, the war memorial, etc., but we were tired after our roistering on the train the night before and it was difficult to concentrate. Orel was occupied and then completely destroyed by the German army. It is now pleasant and wooded and a place where people come to rest and recuperate. However, there was to be no rest for me in Orel. Paul Bailey – who enjoys a spot of kindly mischief making, described me as 'une femme louche' to the writers of Orel, from then on I was pursued. 'Sue', 'Sue' was groaned in my ear at frequent intervals by a Siberian playwright. A small humpbacked poet was constantly wisecracking at my elbow. My suitors and I conversed in appalling French. 'Merci', I said over and over again as more presents appeared. The small poet had demonic powers. On a visit to the Turgenev estate – an enchanting place where the ground is covered in wild flowers and there is a lake with two rotting Billy Goat Gruff bridges – I was led towards the woods by him and two more swains, one of whom had a bottle of wine concealed in his briefcase. Only the pop-socked guide prevented a fate worse than watching Rolf Harris in concert. My silent appeals for help had been ignored by my crouching, laughing compatriots.

A rock band played as we ate dinner in the Shipka, people danced, there was a quarrel over a woman, a near fight. Melvyn Bragg was playing the guitar in an apathetic fashion. A sulky blonde glamorous girl sang. Then at nine o'clock everything closed down, so we went to my room and performed *Private Lives* on the balcony and got bitten by mosquitoes and drank cheap champagne. Craig Raine laughed loudly until the early hours, and kept Timothy Mo awake.

The gods punished Paul Bailey; he had a bad reaction to the mosquitoes and was ill for four days. I was very sorry for him as I had grown to like him enormously.

We retreated back to Moscow. We arrived at 6.30 in the morning. Even at this early hour Russia was on the move, the station was jam-packed full. We passed through a massive waiting room where every plastic chair was occupied, yet nobody spoke. Christopher Hope was much affected by this. It was in complete contrast to the milling, shouting crowds outside with their ungainly luggage and wool-wrapped children in tow. There was one policeman at the door – could he alone have cowed hundreds of people into complete silence?

We went to the Bolshoi and saw the most exquisite dying swan, performed by Ms Larissa, the toast of Moscow, who was reputed to be rushing towards sixty years of age. Her arms vibrated like piano wires, they shimmered, then as the violins soared and swooned she sank to the floor in the final gesture – it was perfect and lovely and I shall always remember it.

I arranged to meet my translator, but he mixed up Tuesday with Thursday so it was not possible. He is translating a *diary*. As Mr Bennett said, 'Friday: Got up, went to Sunday School.'

We were invited to Kim Philby's funeral and said we'd go, but the day was changed and we'd flown to Lvov in the Ukraine. We met more writers and admired the beautiful town and visited the cathedral which was crowded with old women, many on their knees. The sadness was tangible. It was Ascension Day and a kindly old woman began to explain the story of the Ascension to Alan Bennett.

Alan listened as though the story were completely new to him. Then an *unkind* old woman intervened and ordered him to uncross his legs. She then turned on the kind old woman and berated her for talking to us. Later, strolling round the town, we saw the unkind woman praying at the locked gates of a church. She looked very unhappy. We met the mayor of Lvov, a big, handsome man, very conscious of his duty to preserve and renovate the many lovely buildings with which the town is blessed. Alan Bennett is thinking of retiring to Lvov. We met a dirty, ragged man who told us about the concentration camp which used to be situated to the west of the town. Hundreds of thousands of people died there. I asked our official guide about the old man. 'He is a fanatic', she said. 'He has spent his life since the war studying the fate of the Jews. He is a Jew himself', she added, 'a professor of history.' She disapproved of the ragged old man.

The writers of Lvov were particularly kind and hospitable, and we lunched in some style to the sounds of a string quartet – all girls who blushed when we applauded. The conversation at Messrs Raine, Bennett & Bailey's end of the table had turned to sex. Their laughter attracted the attention of the wife of the chairman of the Lvov Writers Union. I said, 'They are talking about sex.'

'Oh', she said. 'All say's, little do's.'

Quite a devastating remark from such a mild looking woman.

On the flight back Timothy Mo reproduced the sound of the aircraft emergency signal in Mr Bennett's ear. Mr Bennett was already in a lather because a woman sitting in front of him had tried to pull down the emergency exit lever, in order to hang her cardigan on this convenient peg. After such provocation Mr Bennett turned to Mr Mo and said, 'Oh ———— off back to Hong Kong, you slant eyed git!' Mr Mo laughed immoderately, he can give it out and take it back. Mr Mo won't like me saying this, but he is a very kind man. Mr Raine, master of erotic verse, longed for his family in England. Mr Bailey, comedian manqué, missed his dog. Mister Bennett dismissed his label of genius and wished he could dance, and Mr Hope gravely observed the tragi-comedy of Russia and made plans to return. Anne Vaughan and her terrific husband Andy (a dab at changing film in cameras) were returning to the trauma of house-moving.

I fell in love with all five of my companions at different times and for different reasons. I hope that they will understand better than anybody that this attenuated account of our Russian trip is biased, inaccurate and is only my version of the truth. There are five other versions and I look forward to reading them almost as much as I look forward to returning to Russia.

Why I Like England

I like living in England because everywhere else is foreign and strange. The only language I speak is English: I dropped French at school and took up hurdling with the athletic team instead. Even now, in later years, my instinctive reaction on hearing French is to jerk one leg in the air and propel myself towards low garden walls. But I wouldn't like anyone to think that I don't like Abroad. I do. Abroad means adventure and the possibility of danger and delicious food, but Abroad is also tiring and confusing and full of foreigners who tell you that the bank is open when it's not.

Being an atheist I am naturally interested in English churches, and being a town dweller I passionately love the English countryside. Though I will concede that 'it looks better on the telly than it does in real life', as a child new to the countryside said to me once on a Social Services outing.

I only fully appreciated the varied nature of the English countryside after driving for two days through a Swedish pine forest. By the morning of the second day, desperate for novelty, I started counting the dead reindeer that littered the verges. By the afternoon I'd stopped feeling sorry for the reindeer, and by late evening I'd also stopped feeling guilty about owning *two* pine dressers. In fact my first thought on seeing the oak dressers appearing in Habitat's window was that Terence Conran must have been to Sweden on a motoring holiday, and on returning to England had issued a terse memo: 'Pine is out, oak is in!'

I like English weather; like the countryside it's constantly drawing attention to itself. I started this article in a room filled with piercing sunlight, but now a strong wind has materialised and the room is full of gloom.

I like the reserve of English people, because *I* don't particularly want to talk to strangers in trains either, unless of course there is a *crisis* such as a 'cow on the line' causing an hour's delay. In which case my fellow passengers and I will happily spill out our life stories to anybody we can get to listen.

I like the way in which the English cope with disasters: cut our water off and we will cheerfully queue at a stand pipe in the snow. Throw us into rat-infested foreign jails and we will emerge blinking in the daylight to claim that our brutal-looking jailers were 'decent sorts who treated us well'. I bet somewhere, pinned onto a filthy prison wall, is a Christmas card; 'To my friend and captor, Pedro, from Jim Wilkinson of cell 14'.

The England I love best is, of course, the England of childhood; when children could play in the street without the neighbours getting up a petition. When children lisp, 'Tell us about the olden days', I romanticise about the fields and hedgerows, and about the time when a car coming down the unadopted road brought us out of our prefabs to gawp and speculate. I'm happy to live in a country that produces important things: wonderful plays, books, literature, heart surgeons, gardeners and 'Private Eye'. I was asked to write about why I like England in 700 words. Now if I'd been asked to write about why I *don't* like England I'd have needed 1,000, and I suspect it would have been easier to write. It's our birthright and privilege to criticize our own country and shout for revolution. I asked a friend of mine where, given the choice and enough money, he would choose to live. He replied gloomily, 'There isn't anywhere else'. Another friend when asked if she'd ever go on a World Cruise said, 'No, I'd rather go somewhere nice.'

Given the choice between death and exile I'd choose exile every time, but I'd be very, very unhappy at having to leave the club.

Margaret Hilda Roberts

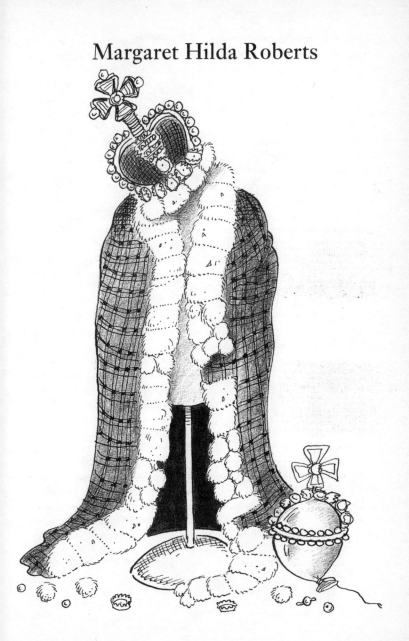

The Secret Diary of Margaret Hilda Roberts Aged 14¼

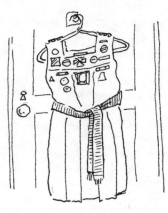

Friday   May 6th

Father has cleverly seen a gap in the lavatory paper market; illiterate households don't buy newspapers, so father is selling ready-strung bundles at a penny farthing each. The first consignment went on sale at 8am and was sold out by 12.30pm. Mrs Arkwright bought six bundles explaining: 'My little 'uns 'as all got the runs through the 'oles in their boots'.

A traveller from London called in for an ounce of shag and passed on a rumour he had heard that a future socialist government would introduce free milk to schools. Father went the colour of barley and had to sit down. When he recovered he said to me: 'The socialists are out to ruin the small shopkeeper, Margaret'. I said: 'But father, you'll be all right, you are over six feet tall'. The traveller and father laughed, I don't know why. If the filthy socialists ever do take power I shall refuse to drink free school milk. If the poor cannot afford to buy it then they must go without.

Saturday   May 7th

Angela Pork-Cracklin had sent a message to the shop asking if I would make up a four in the mixed doubles to be held this evening on her parents' court. Father was delighted (he has been after the Pork-Cracklins' Earl Grey order for years). I told Father that I didn't know how to play tennis. But he took his apron off and ran to the library, returning with Fundamentals of Lawn Tennis. Mother was told to run a tennis dress up on the Singer and, between customers, father and I practised a few strokes using biscuit tins as raquets and stale rock cakes as balls. By four o'clock I had perfected serving to the base line (the bacon slicer) and was working on my back hand, when Mother brought my tennis dress in to be fitted. She spoilt everything by shouting 'Just look at all this 'ere mess. There's crumbs and currants all over my clean shop floor'. Father remained calm. He simply sent Mother into the back room to whiten my plimsols. By six o'clock I had memorised the rules of lawn tennis, and by 7.30 I had beaten Angela Pork-Cracklin six-love six-love. Angela ran into the big house and refused to come out for mixed doubles so they were abandoned and I lost my chance to bring up the subject of the Earl Grey order.

Father was tearing newspaper into squares when I arrived home. We sat and discussed my triumph. Mother joined us while she unpicked the tennis dress for dusters. Thus the time before bed was spent very pleasantly.

Sunday   May 8th

Up at 5am. Did two hours of delicious mathematical equations then woke mother and ordered her to prepare breakfast. Honestly, she is such a slug-a-bed. She would stay in bed until *7.30am* if I let her!

Chapel and Sunday school in the morning, then dinner (*Lunch, Margaret, Lunch!*) followed by afternoon Sunday school, high tea and evening chapel. An ordinary Sunday except for an extraordinary incident when mother was caught red-handed breaking the Sabbath. Yes, at four o'clock I walked into the back room and saw Mother cleaning her shoes. I called father at once and he came downstairs and witnessed mother with the Cherry Blossom in one hand and the polish rag in the other. She begged forgiveness but father was not to be swayed and he forbade her to accompany us to evening chapel. Her absence is sure to cause tongues to wag amongst the congregation but rules are rules and are meant to be kept. All else is anarchy.

Monday   May 9th

Hurrah! Another week of school begins. There is a new girl in our class. Her name is Edwina Slurry. She is obviously ambitious, but she'll have to work jolly hard to knock me from my position at the top of the class. I have asked Mother if I can stop wearing a Liberty bodice. The buttons are an awful nuisance when one is dressing after games. She is going to confer with father and let me know.

Tuesday   May 10th

I have been to see the head to ask if I can be excused from Art. All that messing about with paint and paper is a sheer waste of time, especially when I could be working. Miss Fossdyke said: 'Margaret, the function of Art is to develop the sensibilities, and you of all the girls in my school need to do this as a matter of urgency'. I can't think what she meant by her remarks as I am easily the most sensible girl in the school.

Wednesday   May 11th

Edwina Slurry has been toadying to a disgusting degree. Some of the more impressionable girls have taken to walking arm-in-arm in the corridors with her.

Lady Olga Wasteland lectured the whole school this afternoon. Her subject was 'The Horrors of War'. She related how horrified she was when she realised that fully fashioned nylons were no longer in the shops.

Thursday   May 12th

Methodist Youth Club was spoiled by a fight involving the Prior gang and Cecil Parkhurst's friends. The tea urn was knocked over and the sugar bowl was broken. I think it is time the Prior gang was banned. They have caused nothing but trouble since they became members. Cecil behaved liked the gentleman he is by escorting me out of the hall and seeing that Prior and his bully boys did not bother me.

Was rather upset when I got into bed so I indulged myself in reading my favourite page from *Higher Mathematics Book Four*. The problem 'XXYYZZ = ZZYYZZ, discuss' never fails to make me laugh out loud. However, life can't be all pleasure so I put out the light, repeated 'The rain in Spain falls mainly on the plain' two hundred times and went to sleep.

Friday   May 13th

Dearest diary, without Cecil my life has no meaning, no direction. How I miss him. O Cecil! If only a way could be found to slot you back into decent Grantham society. Meeting illicitly over your weekly Brylcreem order isn't enough for me. Why will no one tell me your crime? What was it exactly you did? Must finish now as it is midnight and father and I are about to do the stock-taking. Mother has already slunk off to bed with a cup of Ovaltine. She is only working a sixteen-hour day. She is not pulling her weight. I will speak to father tonight.

3am. Just back from the woods where Cecil is hiding. I gave him his Brylcreem and was rewarded by a limp handshake; at least I think it was his hand I was shaking; it was too dark to see properly.

Saturday   May 14th

I am in disgrace. Father has found out about the missing jars of Brylcreem. How foolish I was to think he wouldn't notice. In his rage father accused me of having an affair with Arnold Arkwright, who plasters the stuff on his hair with a trowel. I was in the middle of counting the hundreds and thousands cake decorations, and was so upset by father's unjust accusation that I lost count and had to start again. It was 5am before I got to bed.

Sunday   May 15th

Father was awfully stern in the pulpit today. He railed against professional churchmen who insist in meddling in politics. (A guarded reference to Monsigneur Kent who is petitioning the council for a street lamp in Church Lane.) After Sunday dinner I gave father the money I have been saving up for the elocution lessons. I said 'Father, this is to pay for the purloined Brylcreem'. He said 'I appreciate the gesture, daughter, but keep the money, you must acquire a slight lisp if you want to get on in the world'.

Mother said, 'I think it's more important to learn to roll your Rs'. Then she ran giggling into the back room with her apron over head. Father and I looked at each other baffled.

Monday   May 16th

Everybody is being perfectly horrid to me at school. I've been to the headmistress to complain but even she was unsympathetic. She said 'You're overworking, Roberts, I want you to take a few days off.' I protested that the school couldn't function without me'. The head snapped, 'Go home Roberts, and give this note to your parents'.

Dear Mr and Mrs Roberts,
Margaret's behaviour has been giving me great cause for concern. At all times she is neat, clean and controlled. She works prodigiously hard. She is top of every subject barring Art (which, as you know, she sees no point in doing). She is highly competitive on the sports field, is an excellent needlewoman and always wears highly polished shoes. Indeed she is the type of girl one ought to be proud of; but Margaret is wearing out my staff with her constant requests for more work. She is already ink, milk, and register monitor. Class, sports and house captain. She works in the greenhouse during her playtimes and has offended

the school's groundsman by marking out the school hockey pitch during her dinner break. This morning I came into school early and found her mopping out the lavatories. All very laudable, you may think, but her mania for work is making her very unpopular with the other girls. Are there problems at home? Is she compensating for some lack of affection or attention on your part? I'm sorry to worry you with all this but I sometimes fear for Margaret's future. She is an ambitious and clever girl but she must learn to tolerate those of us who are rather more fallible.

Headmistress, Kesteven and Grantham Girls School

P.S. By the way, have you any of those walnut fancies in stock? If you have please bag two separate quarter pounds. I will call into the shop on Wednesday at 4.59pm. to collect them. (Please arrange for Margaret to be in the back room, out of sight.) Thanking you in advance.

Father's hands trembled as he bagged the walnut fancies. He said 'Geniuses are never recognised in their own land.'

Mother suggested an outing to the fairground tomorrow night. I don't want to go but father insisted that mother be chaperoned so I consented.

Tuesday   May 17th

The fairground was full of smelly, working-class oiks enjoying themselves. Mrs Arkwright's lodgers, Ginger Shinnock and Roy Batterfree were trying their strength against Big Benn the strong-man. Big Benn watched their efforts with a supercilious smile. Skinnock and Batterfree were advised by Big Benn that there was only one way to ring the bell and that was to gather all of your strength and then let the hammer fall on the target. Gormless Howe, the village idiot, was driving around the dodgem track in a random and dangerous manner, bumping into other cars. A fairground worker leapt on the back of his car and steered him safely to the side. Poor half wit, his mother shouldn't let him out on his own. I left mother shrieking her head off on the Big Wheel and crept into Madame Du Cann's tent to have my fortune told.

Wednesday   May 18th

I'm still reeling from Madame Du Cann's predictions. She said 'Youse going to be the mightiest in the land one day.' I gasped 'The Queen?' 'No, better than Queen', she rasped. I wiped my palms and she continued her scrutiny, but then a look of horror crossed her face. 'What is it?' I cried. 'No! No! 'Tis too 'orrible!' she croaked. 'Get you home, you poor, doomed creature.'

What *else* did she see? I must know.

Thursday   May 9th

I crept from the shop and pounded (difficult to do on canvas) on Madame Du Cann's tent flap. Her swarthy features grimaced as she saw me. Eventually, after silver had crossed hands, she consented to tell me all.

'You will marry a small bald man with weak eyes who will sire you with two babbies from one egg. One will be a she child and will give you no trouble but the other, t'other will be a he child and will grow to be a monster. He will bear the name of a European Currency (Frank?) and after embarrassing you with family planning sponsorship and wandering a desert he will destroy your career. For, and this is the curse, you will love this monster blindly *and will see no wrong in him*'.

She fell, shuddering, on to the card table and I went home to the shop and slept soundly. As if I would ever do THAT with a man, even once!

Friday   May 20th

Woke up at 4am, refreshed after an hour and a half's sleep. Just for fun read *Intermediate Chemistry* and committed to memory the more difficult formulae. However, life cannot, and should not be, one endless round of pleasure, so at 5am rose and went downstairs to the shop and helped father to water down the dandelion and burdock. Out of two dozen original bottles we managed to eke out one dozen more. Father, who is a good Methodist, explained that our actions were perfectly moral, and that Jesus's trick with the loaves and fishes was an honourable precedent.

Saturday   May 21st

A dreadful thing happened today. A country bus collided with Angela Pork-Cracklin's horse, 'Snooty'. The bus overturned and ended up in a turnip field. Poor Snooty bruised a fetlock, also several working-class people were killed and injured. Father and I have sent a card to Angela commiserating with her on the injury suffered by her beloved, pure-bred beast.

The Parish Council elections take place soon, so father thought it would be politic if I visited the injured in the cottage hospital. I telephoned the Matron to inform her of my impending visit but, to my astonishment she advised me not to come. I snapped, 'But, my good woman I have arranged for the local press to be there.'

She said, 'I don't care if the editor of the *bible* is there. My patients are still shocked and are in no condition to receive visitors'.

Father got on the telephone to a member of the hospital board who happens to owe us £5.10 shillings for sweet sherry, and hey presto the hospital doors opened for me. I was photographed with an Arnold Grimbold (double amputation), a Mabel Spiggs (fractured skull) and a Hed Noddy (multiple fractures) and, by accident, a Nigel Lawless (obesity and inflation). The patients did not seem at all grateful to see me or appreciative of my little jokes about the 'horse power' of the bus. I promised to return on Wednesday.

Sunday   May 22nd

Arnold Grimbold committed suicide tonight. He left a note: 'I can't face Wednesday.' This is thought to be a reference to the day his stumps were due to be dressed. What a weakling; Grantham is better off without him. I have asked for the grapes I gave him on Saturday to be returned to the shop.

Monday   May 23rd

Got up at 5am and helped father to water down the vinegar. Screwed the caps back on bottles then had a lovely cold bath.

Walking to school I was almost knocked down by a horrid working-class man on a bicycle. I castigated him severely. He feebly explained that he had momentarily lost concentration due to tiredness after cycling 60 miles looking for work. I pointed out that he had absolutely no excuse for not keeping to the straight and narrow path and took his name. He claimed it was Tebbit, but I have my doubts. He looked awfully shifty, quite peculiar eyes. His sort ought to be forbidden to breed.

After a most enjoyable maths lesson I felt it was my duty as a monitoress to lecture the first years on the importance of having spotless finger nails. One or two started to snivel, so I kept them behind and gave them a jolly good talking to about keeping one's emotion in check.

School dinner (sorry, *lunch*. Will I never get it right?) was unnecessarily extravagant. I counted two sultanas per square inch in the spotted dick. I complained to the school cook but she rudely told me to 'move along' claiming that I was holding up the second helpings queue.

Had to endure a double period of English Literature in the afternoon. I will be pleased when we have finished *Hard Times* by that obvious communist Charles Dickens. I offered to balance the lesson by reading aloud from Queen Victoria's letters but Miss Marmaduke refused and asked me to sit down. (A word in the head's ear world not come amiss: Miss M. is recently back from a cycling tour of Russia.)

As I walked home (alone as usual) I saw the man claiming to be Tebbit messing about on a grass verge and pretending to mend a puncture. He was in the vicinity of Snooty's sumptuous stable, so I felt it was my duty to report the matter to our Bobby on the beat. It is a well known fact that the unemployed are horse stealers. Police Constable Perkins thanked me in his broad Lincolnshire dialect and I continued home.

After a scrumptious home baked tea I settled down to four hours of even more delicious chemistry homework.

After the shop closed I helped father with the accounts. I was horrified to discover that Mrs Arkwright of Railway Buildings owes sixpence for groceries. I made father promise that he would never extend credit again. He said, 'Margaret, the woman is a widow with five children to feed.' I said that by granting her credit he would not be helping Mrs Arkwright to mend her reckless ways. I offered to call on Mrs Arkwright and ask her for the sixpence, but father reminded me that it was nearly midnight and that we still had not chopped and bundled the firewood for the shop. (We are taking advantage of a late BBC weather forecast predicting a cold snap.)

Finally got to bed at 2am, recited 'How now brown cow' one hundred times and will now lay my pencil down and go to sleep.

Tuesday   May 24th

Had a lie in until 6am. Then got out of bed and had a brisk rub down with the pumice stone.

I opened the curtains and saw that the sun was shining brightly. (A suspicion is growing in my mind that the BBC is not to be trusted.)

Father and I hastily split the firewood into toffee apple sticks and Mother was sent into the kitchen to make three hundred toffee apples. Dear diary, I'm rather worried about Mother. She looks more timid and nervous every day. I simply can't think why: she has her baking, her duties in the shop and a full social life with the church, so I don't understand why, whenever I address a remark to her, she twitches and stutters and backs away from me. She has also taken to wearing a large crucifix.

Wednesday   May 25th

Went to see Mrs Arkwright and managed to get threepence farthing out of her. I spent some time on her ill-scrubbed doorstep explaining how she should cut down on household expenses. I told her that one could make excellent substitute tea by boiling dried nettle leaves, for example. Mrs Arkwright said it was a bad day for England when a person couldn't afford a cup of tea, but I retorted that it was the duty of all of us to make sacrifices in order to finance the munitions industry. Mrs Arkwright sarcastically asked what I, as a grocer's daughter, went without. I answered that I had given up applying Vaseline to the sores on my legs caused by my wellington tops rubbing.

Mother simply stank of garlic tonight. Is she turning Catholic?

Thursday   May 26th

Police Constable Perkins called round to the shop to report that the cyclist Tebbit had been held at the Police Station for three days of questioning but had now been released without charge. I was rather put out by this apparent evidence of police laxity, but Perkins said, 'His spokes were in a proper state by the time we'd done a strip search of his bike. So don't worry, Miss Roberts, he won't be riding around no more Lincolnshire lanes a' bothering young ladies. No, he'll be pushing that bike all the way back to London town!'

We all had a jolly good laugh and father invited Perkins to join us in a cup of tea at the side of the bacon slicer. He didn't stay long, because, as he explained, it was the scrumping season, and he was kept busy catching young boys and fracturing their eardrums.

When he had gone, father and I did the daily stocktaking and were shocked to find there was a tin of salmon and a small Hovis missing.

My mother claimed that Constable Perkins had slipped them into his truncheon pocket as he left the shop!

Father sent her to bed for daring to cast a slur on a fine body of men. All the same the loss of the salmon and Hovis was a severe blow. Strict economies would have to be made, so father and I sat up all night grinding chalk and adding it to the flour bin.

Friday   May 27th

Got up at dawn to write an essay on magnetic particles. It was so enjoyable that I got carried away and was almost late for school.

After school dinner (*lunch* Margaret, *lunch*) I was summoned to the head. She astonished me by saying 'Margaret, I can't fault your school work, but please do try to take life *less* seriously, perhaps strike up a friendship with one of the girls in your class.' I pointed out to her that there *were* no girls of my class at the school, but she murmured, 'That isn't quite what I meant, dear,' and dismissed me.

After school I counted and bagged the currants and raisins for the shop, then spent two relaxing hours doing mathematical equations.

There was a church social at the Methodist Hall so I took a pound of broken bourbons that father had donated and spent the evening chatting to a visiting Russian Orthodox priest. He was awfully handsome and intellectual and I was delighted when he offered to walk me home. We were approaching the shop chatting about samovars when he crushed me to his chest in a bear hug and whispered lewd and revolutionary suggestions of a personal nature. I screamed and ran into the shop. I didn't tell father, but I will never trust another Russian as long as I live.

Took a cold water bottle to bed with me to punish myself for stealing a raisin.

Saturday　May 28th

Spent a frustrating morning poring over my school atlas doing Geography homework: locate and then draw the Falkland Islands. After searching the entire coast of Scotland and its environs I happened to glance down at the bottom left hand corner of the map and found them off the coast of Argentina!

Sunday　May 29th

At 7pm I broke my promise to myself and with a trembling hand I closed and locked my bedroom door, took my secret box out of my wardrobe and had a session of dressing up and posing in front of the mirror.

The crown kept slipping down over my head and I had to stop twice and stitch the cotton wool back onto the ermine robe, but I think I have almost perfected the regal wave.

I am now certain that I am of royal birth. I'm grateful that I have been adopted by simple, kindly grocer-folk, but the life of a commoner is not for me. I need to know my *true* lineage.

Dear King,
　　I will get straight to the point, did you or any of your close relations visit Grantham fifteen and a half years ago? And if so, did you or they happen to 'bump' into a plump, pleasant faced, rather simple woman?
　　I ask, sire, because I am the offspring of that good

woman. There is a certain Hanoverian cast to my features which does not correspond to any other branch of the 'family' physiognomy.

To be blunt: I am convinced I am of Royal birth. At present I am living with good, decent grocer-folk but 'tis with your family I belong, sire. I know you are a busy man but I would appreciate an early reply; my future depends on it. By the way, you can count on my complete discretion. There is no danger of me blabbing our secret to friends – I have no friends.

I sign myself,
Margaret Hilda Roberts
(until you inform me otherwise)

P.S. Should you need to order ceremonial robes etc., I am a size 14 with my Liberty bodice, size 12 without.
P.P.S. Should I start having riding lessons? If so should I ride side-saddle or should I straddle the horse?

Monday   May 30th

Dearest Diary,

Poor father has been inundated with complaints about his food. Mrs Arkwright came into the shop this morning and claimed that 'Your eggs is all rotten, Roberts'.

Her course working class accent grated on my ears and she went on, 'An' I ain't surprised, seeing as how youse chickens is all scabby and mangy an' is fed on fish 'eads.'

She was joined by Mrs Pork-Cracklin who accused father of selling diseased cheese. In more refined tones she complained, 'My dinner guests have telephoned me this morning – from their respective lavatories, to inform me that they suspect your cheese to be the cause of their lavatorial incarceration'.

Father got rid of Mrs Arkwright by threatening to inform the authorities that she keeps lodgers. However, he was extremely unctuous to Mrs Pork-Cracklin – he gave her a box of iced fancies and a tin of Earl Grey. Then, he dropped to his knees and begged her forgiveness. She generously gave him absolution before sweeping out of the shop and climbing into her limousine.

Tuesday   May 31st

I received the following note from Cecil this morning:

> The Little Hut
> The Woods
> The Wilderness

Mags old girl,
    I say, do you think you can deliver another jar of
Brylcreem to me tonight? This 'living in the open' business
is playing havoc with my hair. Also, Mags sweetie, could
you put in a good word for me with the Grantham worthies
– I'm most awfully fed up with living in the actual and
metaphoric wilderness. Surely I have paid the price for my
little slip up last year. It proves I have red blood in my
veins (and lead in my pencil) doesn't it? I steered the
Methodist Youth Club to victory in our last election didn't
I? Without me you could be languishing on the sidelines –
making the tea, instead of enjoying high office as
Chairwoman (Youth Wing).
    Well, old girl, must stop now, I have to bathe in the
stream and later rebuild my little hut which blew down in
the night.
              Yours with love and devotion
              Cecil Parkhurst

P.S. Could you make it a *large* jar?

Wednesday   June 1st

I saw Cecil tonight! We sat inside his crude hut illuminated only
by the candle I had slipped inside my knickers. He told me the
whole sordid story: how he had been cruelly seduced by a girl
who, instead of doing the decent thing and going to Switzerland
for nine months, had stayed in the district and paraded her shame
for all to see. Cecil, poor pet, had subsequently been banished
from Grantham (father has forbidden his name to be mentioned
in our shop).
    I swore to Cecil that I would not rest until he was re-instated

into some high office in the Youth Club. I asked what other skills
he possessed.

He said, 'Well I used to be quite good at tinkering about with
the electrics on my Hornby train set'.

Thursday   June 2nd

Mother was seen hob-nobbing with Mrs Arkwright this morning;
they were admiring each others' aprons. Father warned her
against getting too familiar. He said, 'As a Christian you have
a duty to avoid the ungodly.'

Mother replied, 'Oh go and stick your head in the pickle barrel
you stuck up prat!'

And this in front of Mrs Arkwright! Father sent mother
upstairs immediately. After she had slammed the bedroom door
he turned to me and said, 'Let this be a lesson to you Margaret,
steer well clear of the working classes. Not only do they pollute
the air they also have a deleterious affect on the vocabulary.'

This evening in my role as Chairwoman of the Methodist
Youth Club I proposed that Cecil be given the job of rewiring the
premises – he would be Head of Electricity. There were a few
grumbles but the motion was carried and a runner (Wriggley
Ridley) was sent to inform Cecil that his period in the wilderness
was over.

Friday   June 3rd

Mother has gone on strike. She stayed in bed all day reading
Madame Bovary and eating violet creams. Nothing father said or
did would shift her. She is demanding a wage for her work in the
shop! I fear this is a sign of madness. She will surely end up in
the Grantham Insane Asylum. This is tragic for us all. Father
may have to *employ* somebody to help in the shop *and* keep the
house. And how will we afford the bus fare to the lunatic asylum
once a week?

Saturday   June 4th

Mother has come to her senses. She was downstairs as usual this
morning. Her day of insurrection has not been mentioned.

Sunday   June 5th

Glancing through the accounts I noticed a new entry: 'Mrs Roberts, wages: sixpence a week'.

So, father has capitulated to industrial action has he? How despicable! That is something I would never *ever* do.

We have not yet had a reply from the King. We are most displeased. When we are Queen we will remember this insult. We will take our revenge on our royal relations. The Throne! The Throne! The Throne!

Correspondence of a Queen in Waiting

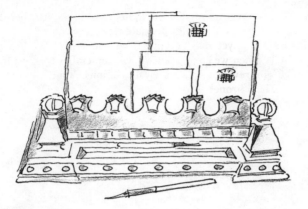

Dear Claire,

We are a woman of sixty plus years old, married to a man much older than myself. Our children have long fled from the nest. I have a demanding and fulfilling full time job. I live in several comfortable homes. My social life is rich and varied and I travel the world and meet interesting, powerful people. I have a very posh accent and am terribly *good* at things.

My problem is this. Nobody likes me. I know this for a fact. Wherever I go people grovel and fawn and smile to my face, but they do this out of fear; their eyes show their terror.

I am *so* unhappy, Claire; what do you advise?

Size Fourteen of Westminster.

Dear Size Fourteen,

Well, well, well. You are in a dither aren't you? Is there a possibility that you have halitosis, or an offensive body odour? Or perhaps you are *too* good at things. How about a public failure? Have you considered coarsening your accent? You say your husband is much older than yourself. Does this mean that you have ceased to have a warm, loving relationship? If so why not try awakening his desires? There are some wonderful multi-

coloured condoms on the market now, any of which would
add pep to your marriage bed.

Claire.

Dear Claire,
1: Four Metropolitan Police sniffer dogs have examined me for
halitosis and body odour. All four pronounced me odour free.
2: I have already *tried* public failure: four million people are
unemployed in this country.
3: I occasionally forget myself and coarsen my posh accent in
the heat of debate.
4: I sent for the condoms and gave them to my husband;
saying, 'for the bedroom dear'.
He blew them up and hung them over the bed.

What *am* I to do?

Size Fourteen of Westminster.

Dear Size Fourteen,

I now know who you are. If you want friends you must
resign. There is no alternative.

Claire.

Dear Earnest Eggnogge,

How dare you waste my time; don't you know I am a *de
facto* royal personage? I've received some whining, snivelling,
wipe my eyes, pass the Kleenex letters in my time, but yours
truly takes the Huntley and Palmers. Quite frankly, I don't give
a toss that your old mother died of hypothermia last winter or
that your zit-faced, moronic teenaged lout of a son has not
worked since leaving school. And the news that your wife has
been waiting for six years to have her nasty, infected womb
removed left me cold. Haven't you got a sharp knife, for God's
sake? Show some initiative, man, borrow a surgical handbook
from the library (be quick, I'm thinking of privatising them),
scrub the kitchen table, put your wife on her back and delve in
there. (Wash your hands first.)

In your horrible working class handwriting you inform me

that your stinking lavatory pan has been leaking for over a year and that rats regularly cavort in your living room. Can't you see the obvious solution, you contemptible prole? Train the rats to do simple tricks – jumping over cans of baked beans, etc., charge the public an entrance fee to goggle at the spectacle and with the proceeds you can stroll around a bathroom supplies centre and nonchalantly order yourself a whole bathroom suite, should you so wish.

You dare to say that I am out of touch with 'real people' and suggest that I 'jump on a train and come up North'.

Firstly, Mr Eggnogge, I am married to a 'real person'. Dennis is, contrary to appearances, neither a robot, nor an extraterrestrial being, nor an aqueous creature who crawled out of a deep lake.

Secondly, I would rather spend the night with Guy the Gorilla (yes, I know he's dead) than climb aboard one of those vile, rattling contraptions and visit you all up there in slag heap land. We have nothing in common. I hate ferrets, dripping, pigeons, corner shops and fat, ugly pale people who are unable to speak in complete sentences and who don't understand how the International Monetary Fund works.

Finally, at the end of your letter you bleat on about your dole payment, calling it a 'pittance' and an 'affront to your dignity'. This last bit made me laugh quite a lot. What did you get for Christmas? A subscription to *Marxism Today*?

Listen, parasite, that's the point, don't you see? We don't need you and your sort any more. Get the message now? Take my advice, shovel the coal out of the bath, then fill it up and jump in and drown yourself.

H.M. Thatcher

N.B. *Note to Private Secretary*
Tidy this up a bit will you Rupert?

Dear Mr Eggnogge,
The Prime Minister was most concerned to hear of your difficulties. She is looking in to the various matters you raised in your letter.
Your sincerely,
Rupert Brown Bear.